GINGERDREAD

Leonard and Ann Marie Wilson

ISBN-13: 978-1-7355525-2-1

Library of Congress Control Number: 2021902226

LOST IN THE WOOD PRESS

www.lostinthewoodpress.com

Conway, Arkansas, U.S.A.

DEDICATION

To Ann's big brother, John Belden, who was always willing to be her hero and probably didn't think she was evil. Probably.

ACKNOWLEDGEMENTS

Cover Design by Peter O'Connor
https://bespokebookcovers.com

Copy Editing by Elise Williams Rikard
https://www.elisewilliamsrikard.com

Editorial Assistance provided by
Fellowship of Conway Literati

CHAPTER ONE

Another Brick in the Wall

"Jordan? Is that you?"

Jordan froze as the flame of his lonely little candle guttered in the wind, threatening to abandon him to the dark amid the scorched stonework and partially consumed timbers of the old manor house. A cold sense of dread settled in his stomach, and he cursed his bravado for coming here at all, much less for having called out when he heard the crying.

"Jordan? Honey? The door's stuck. Could you maybe...? Please?"

He couldn't see a door along this stretch of wall even if he'd been inclined to open it. Eva's muffled voice carried faintly through the soot-stained plaster opposite the room's only window. On some other night, the moon might have poured a token illumination through it, but with the current overcast all the window let in was a chill breeze and a bit of drizzle.

"Jordan? Jordan? Please answer me. I can't see anything in here. You're not still mad at me, are you?"

No, he wasn't. Jordan couldn't find his voice, but he wasn't angry. All the anger had drained out of him months ago.

"Please, Jordan?" Eva's voice cracked with the suppressed desperation that had been lurking at its corners the whole time.

"I'm really sorry. Just let me out." Hearing that desperation come to the fore seemed nearly as surreal as the thought of a rabbit reciting epic verse. A high-born lady of noble bearing, Jordan's stepmother had been a commanding, confident presence in his life all the time he'd known her.

In defiance of his racing heart telling him to flee back to the new manor house and the safety of his bed, Jordan reached out hesitantly, his fingertips brushing the wall, probing for any seam or crack his eyes might be missing in the dim light. He'd already walked all the way around this supporting wall.

The thing was stout enough to have room for a crawlspace, but he hadn't found any reason to believe there actually was one. Well, he hadn't found any reason other than the voice. Now even that seemed to have stopped as the long, silent seconds ticked by. No more sobbing. No more pleas. He dared to lean in close, pressing his ear up against the wall. Could he hear breathing? Or was that just his own...

Jordan jumped as the wall shook, then again as the remnant of a beam dislodged from the ceiling crashed down not two arm-lengths away from him. The candle went out. In the darkness, blow after blow hammered against the wall, either from within or beyond, as Eva's voice wailed hysterically. "Jordan? Jane? Garret? Anybody? Let me out let me out let me out! Oh go'ss, let me out!"

Even the bravest 12-year-old has his breaking point. Jordan scrambled to the window, orienting on the rectangle of near-black just visible against the pitch black of the outer wall, and vaulted out of it. He landed badly in the dark, giving a turn to his ankle, and he sprawled in the mud. Not waiting for the pain to sink in, he pulled himself directly to his feet, only to go sprawling once again as the ankle refused to bear his weight. Still feeling nothing through the adrenalin, he tried once more, and this time managed to stay on his feet.

Half hopping, half running, he hurried through the orchard that lay between the half-burned, old manor house and the half-built new one as fast as the dark night—and his injury—would allow. Something snagged at the ankle he hadn't twisted. Sharp and cruel, it cut a bloody line across his flesh, but he didn't stop, didn't slow, didn't look down, didn't look back.

If he looked back and didn't see the nightmare visions that were chasing him, he'd keep imagining they were there, just out of sight, in the darkness. If he did look back and see them, well...Jordan was old enough to have learned that half the trick to being brave was not letting yourself think about what a hopeless mess you'd gotten yourself into; and if he surrendered another ounce of bravery he'd melt into a puddle on the ground.

The glimmer of another candle ahead signaled that Jordan had broken out of the trees. Jane was waiting for him, holding the candle aloft in the nursery window as she peered out into the night, trying to see him. The thought of his little sister seeing him in such a state wedged itself in Jordan's mind enough for the panic to fray around the edges, and he started actually listening again.

There were no sounds of pursuit. The hammering and the wailing had either stopped or else faded to nothingness from the distance. Finally, Jordan risked a look back. Seeing nothing, he slowed, and the fear of Jane seeing him in such a state began to edge its way up in volume to compete with the fear that had set him running.

Admitting fear to a younger sibling had no place in the big brother code of honor. He might have wet himself, but the upside of having sprawled in the mud was that no one would notice.

"Did you find the screech owl, Jordan?" Jane called down quietly.

He'd assured her that the screams they'd heard in the night were just a screech owl. Sibling bickering and posturing had ensued until she'd wound up maneuvering him into either going out to look for the owl or admitting to both ignorance and cowardice.

"No," Jordan admitted. "I never found the owl. Just a bear. It ate my candle."

Where a part of the new manor house remained under construction, Jordan climbed the workman's scaffolding to a lower section of roof and carefully crossed the slate tiles to where he could edge along the upper wall to the nursery window.

"Nuh-uh you didn't," Jane accused, though he could see the credulity in her eyes. She wanted to believe, so he obliged.

"Did too," he said matter-of-factly. "It was kind of a small bear, but gruff and growly and it ate my candle, so I bopped it on the nose. We wrestled." He gestured down at his muddy clothes. "It got away."

Another little sister might have seized the opportunity to tell him about the trouble he'd be in for getting muddy, but Jane wouldn't have been fooling anyone. Father didn't care and this time there was no maiden aunt hanging around to scold him. Jane's eyes just widened instead, imagining the epic battle. Those eyes were the only thing about her that reminded Jordan of Calista, Jane's mother. Jane had gotten her dark hair and slender face entirely from their father.

Jordan stripped off his muddy tunic and cleaned up at the wash basin, debating with himself over whether to mention anything about Eva. He desperately wanted to tell someone, but Jane wouldn't believe the real bits about Eva, and that would beg scrutiny of the made-up bear story. The whole thing would unravel. He liked the bear story. No, he couldn't tell Jane about

Eva. There were limits to what one could confide in a little sister.

"Jordan, you're getting blood on the floor!" Jane sounded suitably awed.

"Stupid bear," he said in a showy grumble. He moved the wash basin to the floor so he could sit down and wash his bloodied ankle too. "Go cut me a sleeve off something?" He managed to hide his grimace until the 8-year-old had hastened to comply.

As the adrenalin ebbed, this was really starting to hurt. It didn't look pretty, either. The wound appeared to be shallow, but it was jagged. Would it heal clean? He doubted it. Well, there were worse things than having a scar to show along with your stories of wrestling a bear in the night.

So if he couldn't tell Jane, could he tell anyone? There wasn't a grown-up in the world who would believe him.

He'd go back in the morning and listen at the wall to prove to himself that he hadn't just left his stepmother to die. It was true he'd never seen her body after the fire. No one would let him. But even if she hadn't really died in the fire, it had been over a year—and she'd called out to him as if they'd been talking just yesterday.

Once his wound was bound and he was in a clean nightshirt, Jordan chased his sister off to bed—partly because it was the thing to do, but mostly so he could let the mask drop and do a little crying over the pain and the fright.

He really missed Calista right now. She'd just been his stepmother before Eva, but he couldn't remember his own mother; so she was the closest thing he had. She'd been the good stepmother. Eva had been the bad. Jordan couldn't even be sure which thing Eva would expect him to still be mad at her for among all the reasons she'd ever given him to be angry. The last one he could remember was when she'd backhanded Jane so hard it knocked her off her feet.

Like every little sister ever, Jane could be profoundly annoying, but she was still his little sister who Calista had left him as his remembrance of her. Sometimes he was jealous that Jane was Calista's flesh-and-blood daughter, but sometimes Jane was jealous that Jordan was old enough to remember Calista, so on the whole it balanced out.

Anyway, if he'd had a chance to walk away and leave Eva locked in a closet that day, Jordan probably would have taken it; but the option never presented itself. Instead he'd stewed for a week, concocting and dismissing elaborate revenge plans— most of which involved the spiders he knew she hated. Then the fire came, and it burned away the revenge fantasies along with the stepmother.

He'd never wanted her dead. She'd never been that bad. He'd just wanted her far, far away, where she never would trouble them again. Jordan had hurt people before, and it had never made him feel better. Mostly it just made him feel worse—even when they'd been asking for it—so he'd matured now to the point that his idea of revenge generally involved the unexpected introduction of creepy-crawly things. Hitting his sister was more than arachnid-worthy, but it didn't rise to the level of "burned alive".

Somewhere out in the night, the distant shriek that had started all this came again. The nursery, without a candle burning, was no brighter than the old manor house had been, but Jordan didn't have to see his sister to know that the sound had brought her sitting up in bed again.

"It's an owl, Jane," he chided her in his best long-suffering-brother voice, but he hadn't entirely convinced himself of that, even the first time they'd heard it. Now no amount of posturing could blind him to his own doubts. He pulled the covers up tight around him but waited for the sound of Jane's breathing to level out into sleep before allowing himself the luxury of pulling the pillow over his head. He lay awake for a long time, listening to Eva's desperate pleas replay themselves ceaselessly in his head.

Even once he fell asleep, it was a restless sleep full of dark dreams. Sometimes Eva continued to call for help. Sometimes it was Jane. Sometimes it was their father. Once it was his own mother, trapped inside the portrait that had hung in the old house, screaming as the fire consumed it. He woke repeatedly, and when finally it was to find the muted morning sun creeping in around the shutters he quietly rose and dressed himself and slipped back out of the house.

The grounds were already alive with servants hurrying about their chores. He worried at first that the limp he'd earned in the night might attract their curiosity, but none of them spared him a glance.

The presence of the servants had stopped being a novelty, but Jordan could still vaguely remember the before time when he'd been the son of an artisan instead of the son of a baron. Calista had been a baroness. Apparently those didn't generally go around marrying artisans all the time, but his father had been special—was special—a master whose work graced three cathedrals and whose intricate carvings adorned the chapel on this very estate. Calista had admired his piety as much as his talent.

As he neared the burned-out house, Jordan pulled the little lion figurine out of his pocket and clutched it to his chest like a talisman. Calista had given it to him. Though just one of many gifts, it was the last thing she'd ever given him. It had been carved for her out of tiger's eye by his own father. "For my brave little lion," she'd said. "Look after our Jane while I'm gone." He wasn't convinced she'd approve of the job he'd done, but he hoped the fact Jane was still alive would count for something.

The morning didn't hurry to brighten. The overcast and the spring drizzle had lingered from dusk 'til dawn and still showed no signs of breaking. Jordan couldn't have said which window he'd dove out of in the night, but finding the torn-up ground where he'd landed in the mud wasn't hard.

He peered cautiously in through the window there. Beyond lay a smallish room, half-intact but stripped of furnishings, marred by soot and smoke and by a year of partial exposure to the elements. In the dark it had seemed dreadfully sinister. In the morning it just felt abandoned and forlorn. No crying, pleas, or pounding came from within. He wanted to tell himself he'd dreamed the whole episode, but the charred timber lying freshly shattered on the floor said otherwise.

Rather than climb through the window—which looked structurally unsafe—Jordan retraced his steps around to the doorway and through the old house. Whatever the room had been before the fire, he didn't recognize it. This would have been servants' territory and nowhere he had ever ventured. With the scent of damp and decay filling his nostrils, he moved slowly, carefully, so as not to cause any further shifting of the ruin. He also moved as quietly as he was able so as not to disturb anything that might be lurking. Locating the wall, he circled it again, hoping sunlight would reveal something that candle light hadn't. It didn't.

Jordan had longed to find some way to quiet his conscience that didn't involve drawing attention to himself again, but soon it would be breakfast, and lessons would come after that whether he'd eaten or not. Before he could return here again it would almost certainly be dark.

His mind raced down all the possible paths he might find himself on if he walked away not knowing. It didn't like any of them one bit. He weighed them against what could go wrong if he didn't just walk away. It didn't make him feel any better.

How on earth had anyone decided that he was the brave one? But somehow now that everyone thought he was, he was terrified of letting on that he wasn't.

He pressed his ear to the wall again, ready to flinch away and run. Nothing. He closed his eyes. He drew a deep breath. He realized he was stalling. He rapped quietly on the wall. He rapped again a little louder.

"Hello?" The voice came small, tentative.

"Eva?" he finally managed to squeak, emboldened by the morning light.

"Jordan? Jordan, please don't go."

He started to say he'd just run to get help, but could he? Maybe if he came up with the right lie. Maybe. "I...I'm not leaving," he said finally. "How can I help?"

"It's so dark. I can't see. The door is stuck."

"Eva, I don't see any door," he said, starting to feel a little better, bolder. A weight had lifted when he focused on her fear instead of his.

"What?! No! It's here. Right here." The distinct rattling of a doorknob could be heard through the wall.

"Rap on the door," he said. "There, by the knob." He heard it. "Keep rapping." With his ear to the wall, he kept listening, moving around until he'd pinpointed the spot. He drove his knuckles into the plaster there, creating a noticeable dent, then he went looking for a makeshift tool.

He found it in the form of a jagged piece of stonework that had fractured from the wall. With it, he began to gouge at the plaster in earnest. It crumbled away quickly and easily, but revealed only solid brick behind.

Jordan honestly couldn't say whether he was disappointed or relieved, but it was too late to walk away—even for breakfast.

It was too late to walk away even if he missed lessons and they sent a search party. If that happened and they didn't hear Eva it would mean the willow switch. If they did hear her, though, then he could pass the whole thing off to the grown-ups. He'd have to risk it.

"Jordan?"

"It's just a wall!" he called back. "I still can't see…" His voice trailed off, and he hurried once more around the wall, inspecting it, his confusion giving way to suspicion.

"Hold on," he said when he got back to where he started, and he began hacking away at the plaster again until he found the vertical seam where red brick met gray stone. Then he tore at it the other direction until he found another seam.

Brickwork less than a yard wide lay between him and his stepmother. Someone had bricked up a doorway and plastered over it. Jordan's stomach tied itself in all sorts of new knots as that fact sank in, then got dragged to new depths as he studied the soot on the remaining plaster. There was no possible way that the door hadn't been sealed off before the fire. His knees gave way to fear and horror, and he started retching on the spot, trying to turn out the contents of an empty stomach.

"Jordan? Jordan? What's happening?"

As the heaving of his stomach finally subsided the plaintive voice kindled a new emotion in Jordan. It was the first embers of anger. No matter what was happening, there was no way on the Goddess' blessed earth it had any right to be happening.

"I need to get something," Jordan said firmly. "I'll hurry as fast as I can. On my mother's grave, I will be right back." Not daring to wait for a response, not even daring to tread lightly through the ruin lest he stop to think and find the anger subsiding, Jordan scurried away as quickly as his ankle would allow. He rushed past startled servants, being the one this time to pay them no notice, and didn't stop until he reached the outbuilding that was his father's old workshop.

Father didn't have the time for the workshop that he used to, and no self-respecting nobleman would work with his hands—but Father said he'd be damned if he'd be a self-respecting nobleman, so it remained open if a bit dusty and disused. The important thing right now was that it contained a nice, sturdy hammer, as heavy as Jordan dared use. Between the burden, his being winded, and the ankle growing angrier again from use, it took Jordan a fair bit longer to get back to the ruin, but he made the best time he could.

He arrived to the sound of muffled sobs. "I'm here!" he called. "Stay back from the door."

Jordan hefted the hammer over his head with both hands. He brought it down on the brick wall with all the strength he could muster. The impact jarred his bones painfully—reminding him there was a technique to swinging a hammer—but it didn't have any noticeable effect on the wall.

He allowed himself a few moments to wallow in the pain until it subsided, then tried again. This time, a little spiderweb of cracks radiated out from the point of impact, but only a couple of inches across.

He hauled back the hammer again and, with a cry that mingled frustration, rage, and determination, spun completely around to build up momentum and hit the wall with all the force he could muster. Brick and mortar fractured. A fragment of something stung his cheek, drawing blood not half an inch from his eye. Dust rained down around him. Timbers complained loudly overhead.

Jordan ignored the pain. He ignored the dust and the creaking. He was afraid the building might finish collapsing on top of him at any moment. He was afraid of what he would find if he broke through. He was afraid he'd be leaving his stepmother to die if he didn't break through. He was afraid of how the adults around him would react to what he was doing. But most of all, he was afraid that if he didn't break through this wall, right here, right now, he would never be able to sleep again.

It was the brickwork that gave first, shattering into chunks that remained mortared together but that he could finally grab and start pulling away. He had to dance away from the first big piece when it nearly fell on him. Heavier than he'd anticipated, it came crashing down on the stone floor right where he'd dropped the hammer and shattered into rubble on top of it. That was okay. He could already see the door to some cramped little closet or pantry—old and dusty but untouched by the elements that had been eating away at the ruin around it.

"Light! There's light!" Eva's voice came excitedly, no longer muffled by the brickwork. At the same time a new smell came rolling through the cracks around the door, as unexpectedly pleasant as it was completely out of place. Warm and sweet and spicy, it steamrolled over the dust, the damp, the mold, and the decay, filling the air with the aroma of hot molasses like...like freshly baked gingerbread? Of all the things he had suspected, expected, and dreaded he'd find, this didn't align with a single one of them.

"Jordan? What's happening?"

He realized he'd stopped pulling at the brickwork. The ruin had fallen silent apart from the distant sounds from the manor. The doorknob rattled. He couldn't see it yet, but he could hear it quite clearly. The door jostled ineffectually against the brickwork still wedged in front of it. Still, it opened a crack. Eva's voice gave a startled little shriek, followed by heavy breathing.

"Eva?" Jordan asked tentatively. He was still trying to work out how gingerbread could smell...sinister.

"You're still out there?" Her voice was shaking.

"Yes. Yes!" He fought down the returning doubt and fear to re-focus his dissipating resolve and tore down another big chunk of brickwork.

"Not..." Her shaking voice dropped so near a whisper he had to strain to hear it. "Not in here?"

Jordan took a step back from the door. When she started to scream, he took a second step and a third. She was still screaming when he paused at the window—aware that he was poised to escape through it again, but just managing to hold himself back as his mind ran once more through possible futures.

He'd feigned bravery enough times to know how fear worked. If he crossed that threshold, he knew he would never come back here. If he never came back, he would never know. If he never knew, he would always be terrified. Always. He would spend his life avoiding dark places, jumping at sounds in the night, and dreading closing his eyes to face yet another round of guilt-fueled nightmares.

At last, he broke the impasse by striking a bargain with his fears and dashed back across the room to start tearing at the brickwork. Big pieces crashed to the floor. Lone bricks got flung aside. When the doorknob came into view, he turned it and pulled, managing to open the door by two or three inches because the knob no longer wedged it closed.

The aroma of hot gingerbread redoubled, hitting him square in the face. The sheer impossibility of that nearly broke him again, but he blanked out his mind and kept working because Eva kept screaming. When the door opened for real, he would be free to run. No matter what opening it revealed, his instincts could take over and his body could have its way. Until then, he worked mechanically.

"Jordan!" Bloodied fingers with worn and broken nails burst through the crack, clawed at the edge of the door. He pretended he didn't see them, pretended he could no longer hear the screams, pretended he didn't notice how the fingers yanked the door forcefully closed on themselves with a sickening crack, then vanished back inside.

He pretended he couldn't hear the sobs now mingled with the screams, or that both began to dwindle as if retreating down some long, echoing corridor. He wasn't even there to notice them. He'd gone somewhere else and left his body to mindlessly pursue the task in front of it.

Then there was no more task, no more screaming. Even the noises of the manor had gone to nothingness. He came back to himself standing in a pile of bricks with the door ajar by a crack. One hand held the knob. His other hand held a brick, raised above his head. He pulled the door open another inch and stood watching, waiting for anything to burst through it. Nothing moved. No sound came. Even the smell had begun to dissipate.

Jordan went to pull the door open another inch and found that he couldn't. Whatever spell he'd cast to bring himself this far had been broken. The link between his will and his hand had been severed. He just stood there, watching, straining to hear anything but his own labored breathing, until he was forced to admit he'd lost this battle and allowed the fear to edge its way out through his body. His hand released the knob. He backed slowly away, never taking his eyes off the door. He was about halfway across the room when the hinges began to creak.

He forced another stalemate with his fear. He'd come this far. He had to see. So he pulled his makeshift weapon back for a throw, quickly bent to grab another in his off hand for more ammunition, and resumed backing toward the window as the door edged open.

The gap slowly grew to maybe half a foot before the wind got proper purchase and flung it the rest of the way open with a bang. Beyond lay an empty closet, not even three feet deep. Empty shelves offered the room's only extension to either side of the door. Jacob couldn't see the back of them from where he stood, but unless they were bizarrely deep, the little room couldn't have been more than six feet wide all told.

Eva wasn't there. No one was there. In fact, the only thing visible in the closet, aside from the shelves, was the glistening spatters of fresh blood scattered randomly about.

Jordan found himself edging closer to the door, then taking great care not to cross the threshold or lower the brick as he verified that the shelves, too, were backed by a featureless wall. He nudged the door closed until it latched, then without consciously deciding to, began piling bricks in front of it to block it closed.

CHAPTER TWO

SICK DAY

"You're a very foolish boy, you know." Despite her words, the priestess's voice wasn't unkind or judgmental. In the hierarchy of maternal figures in Jordan's life, Sister Adalva actually ranked somewhere above Eva and below Calista. She'd been Calista's friend and adviser before becoming his tutor and eventually Jane's, and practically a member of the family before friction with Eva had mostly banished her from the manor house.

For a year or so before the fire, Jordan and Jane had taken their lessons at the soritage, Adalva's cozy little home beside the chapel. Even then, she'd been at least as much of a mother to them as Eva had been.

"Your heart was in the right place, trying to comfort your sister, but going out to hunt a screech owl in the night? You might as well have been chasing a ghost."

Jordan sort of heard her, sort of knew she was there, but he was more aware of the wall next to his bed. The wall was very interesting. The plaster had been painted a pale green. He could find shapes in its texture. The wall was only a few inches deep, with warming daylight on the other side. He'd looked out the window again to make sure before crawling back into bed. He had no idea how long ago that had been, but he'd been studying the wall ever since. It was an interesting wall. Yes.

"Is Jordan all right?"

"Of course, dear." It sounded like Adalva was over by the door now, talking with Jane. "Your brother just caught a chill. Let him rest. You'll have me all to yourself for lessons today, but not while your hair's a tangle and you've still got breakfast jam on your face. Make yourself presentable now. Scoot."

Time passed again. Jordan couldn't say how much, but the light on the wall remained more or less the same, and he recalled only Jane's footfalls scuffing away, not Sister Adalva's.

"Are there real monsters?" he heard himself asking.

"What was that, dear?"

"Are monsters real?" He remained with his back to her, staring at the wall.

"Can't say I've ever met one," Adalva answered him. "Maybe. I don't think so. I suppose it depends on what you call a monster. They make for some fascinating stories, though."

Jordan heard her distinctly not say, "Why do you ask?" He appreciated that.

"Do any of them smell like gingerbread?"

"Well, that's an interesting question and no mistake. I don't know."

He heard the bed creak and felt the mattress give as she sat down behind him.

"What about ghosts?" he asked. "Do ghosts smell like gingerbread?"

"I haven't met any of those, either." He could hear the shrug in Adalva's voice. "I think I heard a ghost carriage once, a long time ago. Heard it very distinctly rattle to a stop outside. Heard the horses snort and stamp. Then...nothing. I went out to look and it just wasn't there."

"Really?" Jordan asked.

"Really. There's weird stuff in the world. Not understanding it can be scary. So we explain it as best we can. If we never get a chance to test the explanation, we declare victory and move on because no one can prove us wrong. It makes the weird stuff easier to take." Adalva's voice paused thoughtfully. "Just a guess, but I think you ran into some weird stuff last night that you haven't been able to explain. That's okay. And if you decide you want to talk to me about it, that's okay too."

Jordan could feel the gears in his head grudgingly rattle back to life and make the effort of considering the offer. Just hearing it made meant a lot. It gave a glimmer of hope he might not have to be alone in...this. In the world of the weird, though, the sounds of a phantom carriage didn't exactly move in the same social circles as what he'd been through, and even well-meaning adults were notorious for their loss of perspective and their mismanaged priorities. For now, he just turned his head slightly and gave a hint of an acknowledging nod.

"When I get back, we'll move you to the healing place, as bad as your chill is," Adalva finally said to his silence. "In fact, go ahead and move yourself if you don't want to risk getting carried around like a sack of potatoes." He could hear the rattle of metal before her shadow fell over him and a key dropped lightly onto the bed between him and the wall.

The "healing place" was a new one on him, but he couldn't stir himself to ask about it. Still, she didn't leave him hanging. "The stair at the back of chapel goes up to the sacristia. That's the safest and most healing space in all the world. All sorts of divine energy collects up there, and I've made myself a little nook by the window where I go when I'm feeling bad." She laid a soft, cool hand briefly on his forehead. "It's a special place I only ever shared with Calista, so don't go blabbing about it, but she'd be the first to tell me you need it."

When she'd gone, Jordan found himself staring at the key, studying it with the same sort of intensity he'd applied to studying the wall. It was a good-sized black key of wrought iron with ivory inlaid into the oblong handle and a circle of deep blue, polished stone set into the ivory in turn. He recognized the stone as one Calista had favored for household decoration and in her everyday jewelry, though he didn't know its name. Taken together with the hole that passed through the circle of blue, the effect created a stylized eye—which would be no coincidence. The watchful maternal eye of Seriena meant protection for the faithful. It would be a fitting key to Sister Adalva's sanctum.

After he stared at the key for a while, he began to fidget with it. After he'd fidgeted with it for a while, he reluctantly slid out from under the covers, pulled on his boots, and began the walk to the chapel. Today, that trip took several times longer than it usually did. The argument could have been made that it was just because he was moving so slowly—partly for his ankle hurting now more than at any point since he'd first turned it—but the distance itself seemed to have elongated in the night.

The chapel sat in the middle of the butterfly garden that had been one of the few things both of Jordan's stepmothers had loved. The transition from winter to spring had barely begun and most of the garden remained so much drab mud beneath a dismal gray sky, but a few floral pioneers had embarked on the process of painting in its glorious colors. In defiance of the chill, a single golden butterfly flitted about the blossoms to land on the wooden memorial statue of Calista that father had carved himself. It was a beautiful thing, smooth and polished and life-like, that had briefly served as the centerpiece of the garden before being moved to a side path beneath the willow tree near the chapel.

The move had roughly corresponded to the arrival of Jordan's second stepmother. That was always one of the things he'd held against her.

While the memorial statue was a thing of beauty, his father's real monument to Calista was the chapel itself—and it was one Eva could never have managed to eclipse if she'd lived to be a hundred. The crowning jewel of the estate could have been the young love child of a cathedral and a palace—not sprawling, but tall and ornate, all stained glass and spires and sacred sculpture.

The chapel of Hollygrove was the envy of every barony in the kingdom and of more than a few counties as well. His father's artistry, Calista's wealth, and their shared piety had achieved their ultimate expression here. It had been mostly done before they'd moved here, when his father married Calista, so it hadn't immediately dawned on Jordan that this wasn't the norm in baronial chapels. It wasn't, though. It really, really wasn't.

The interior of the chapel was no less lavish, but welcoming for all that. Someone else might feel overawed, but to Jordan this was just home. He could look around and see the ghosts of countless family ceremonies and illicit games of hide-and-seek. He could see past the glamor to the accumulated wear of years of use—and in some cases even remember gouging a specific mark in the back of a pew while he was fidgeting or recall swinging from something never designed to support his weight so it had to be replaced. Any chapel was meant to be a sanctuary, but this was his sanctuary.

As he crossed the main floor and mounted the spiraling steps at the back, he could feel some of the weight of his encounter slowly lifting. Maybe he could just sleep in here from now on. It could be the one place in the world he might still escape nightmares.

At the top of the stairs, across from the small choir loft, Jordan found the door to match Adalva's key and he let himself in. Shelves and cabinets that lined the walls housed vestments for Adalva, drapery for the altar, incense, candles, holy books, and other ceremonial artifacts. It was a narrow space but long and crooked, wrapping as it did out of sight around the back of the choir loft. Halfway along, a little fireplace had been built against the inside wall, facing a dormer window seat that looked out on the orchard and the gray sky. A down quilt and several comfy pillows dressed the window seat. Fresh ashes in the fireplace hinted that Adalva had been making use of the nook during the recent rainy days.

Jordan built up a fire and, once it had well and truly caught, stretched out in the window seat where he snuggled gratefully under the quilt. The seat wasn't quite long enough for him to stretch out fully, but he only needed to pull his knees up a bit to fit comfortably. He lay for a moment—staring out the window as a few stray drops of rain pattered lightly against the glass— and had just started to drift off when the burned-out ruin of the old manor house caught his eye, just visible over the orchard. With a small whimper, he rolled around to rest his head at the other end of the bench where the ruin would be out of sight, then he returned to meditating on the sporadic splatter and trickle of the rain drops. Eventually exhaustion overtook him, and he slept.

Jordan knew he'd slept mostly because the light had changed. It had been a mercifully dreamless sleep, and it left him feeling improved enough to doubt his memories. He could start to tell himself the whole thing had been nightmares, even if the effort remained half-hearted and unconvincing. Rather than give himself too much time to dwell on it, he soon roused himself to look for spiritual answers on the nearest bookshelf, hoping that some holy woman would have passed just the insights he needed down through the ages.

To his surprise, he found he'd picked what was probably the only shelf in the room not dedicated to the wisdom of Seriena. Its contents turned out to be a collection of personal journals kept by people he'd never heard of and what seemed to be transcriptions of folklore. Such things might not contain the wisdom of the ages, but they might not be stilted and boring, either. Pulling one down at random, he began skimming through the pages to find out.

An hour later, Jordan had acquired a small pile of books and was still skimming through them from his perch in the window seat. When Adalva had spoken about weird things in the world she'd clearly been thinking about more than a single phantom carriage. These books, which showed the soft wear of careful but frequent handling, probably constituted what Eva would have called the sister's "guilty pleasure". How many hours had Adalva sat on this very spot, he wondered, poring over these tales of the weird, the haunted, and sometimes the unapologetically macabre. That she even kept this collection showed a side of the woman he'd never dreamed existed. As far as he was concerned, it wasn't a good side, it wasn't a bad side, but it was an interesting side. He particularly liked the journals with their first-hand accounts of things whose weirdness ran the gamut from curiosities similar to Adalva's carriage encounter to nightmarish hauntings, to narrow escapes from indescribable monsters. The accounts somehow made him feel less alone.

Struck with inspiration, Jordan searched through the room until he discovered quill and ink and a stash of blank journals. He claimed one, making a mental note to replace it later but unwilling for now to leave the little sanctuary. The demands of his body would make that necessary all too soon. Then he curled up in the window again with the journal in his lap and began writing. If he could tell no one else what had happened he could tell himself, and assuming he chose to share with Adalva at some point, he'd have the details down while he could still remember them properly.

It was nerve-wrackingly cathartic putting the experience into words. By the time Jordan got up to where he was breaching the wall, he could practically smell the warm gingerbread again. Or was he actually smelling it? He stopped and sniffed at the air suspiciously. No. His mind was playing tricks on him. Wasn't it? He couldn't tell. It was so faint but so persistent.

He left off his writing and laid the journal aside to let the ink dry. Was that a distant scratching? The warm little sanctuary no longer felt so warm or so safe. Why had it seemed like a good idea to go off on his own again? He was likely the only living soul in the chapel right now. Jordan closed his eyes, bit his lip, and tried to organize his increasingly chaotic thoughts.

Out of the jumble, he realized he was internalizing two more important lessons about fear: it fed on isolation and it fed on the unknown. When you wall yourself off, he thought—shivering as Eva's screams once more crashed through his mind—you wall fear in with you. In your head, the bad stuff would always be waiting to pounce right there on the other side because you'd never be able to truly conquer it or even to see it leave. Even the mightiest castle had more than one gate to cut down on the chance of your own defenses turning into a death trap.

Resolutely, Jordan returned to his writing, ignoring the taunting of the distant sounds and scents until he was quite done recording his experience. Then he tucked the journal under his arm and left the room, locking it again behind him.

The fear wasn't gone. He still found himself carefully peering around every corner and into every possible hiding place as he made his way back outside, but he got there. By the time he did, the rain had quite stopped, and the sun had begun playing hide and seek from behind the clouds.

When he got to the manor library where Jane was still finishing up her lessons for the day, Jordan caught Adalva's eye and beckoned her out of the room. "Feeling better?" she asked quietly, so as not to disturb Jane's transcription exercise.

"Some," he admitted just as quietly. "Here." Steeling himself, he handed her the journal. "This happened. I don't need you to believe me, but I need to tell somebody. You'll at least find the story interesting even if you think I made it up. If you tell anyone else, or if you ask me even once, I will say I made it up. I'll try to be ready to study tomorrow." Without waiting for a response, he turned and hurried away.

CHAPTER THREE

GHOST STORIES

Most of two years later and most of a foot taller, with the winter snow lying heavy on the ground outside, Jordan sat with the little crowd in the front parlor, listening to Sister Adalva's solstice ghost stories. Continuing in the tradition established by Calista, father always bracketed the night of the winter solstice with two days of feasting for his dozen vassals and their families, and Adalva's tales of the weird and unsettling always proved a popular entertainment.

Adalva had never come out and told Jordan she'd believed his own story. She'd never come out and accused him of anything, either. She'd shown the good grace to be content with the knowledge that he'd believed it. She'd even asked him to show her where it had happened, and in her company he'd found the courage to cross the orchard and return to that place he'd been sure he'd never get close to again.

When they got there, Adalva studied the door and the wall around it intently—clearly intrigued, not just humoring a child. Picking her way carefully through the ruin, she'd asked him to walk her through everything that had happened. She'd posed serious questions about where he'd been standing and about how particular bits of damage to the walls and floor had come about.

At the end, she'd examined the bricks piled in front of the door. "So you did this?" she'd asked. He'd nodded. "Very sensible," she'd concluded. And that had been that.

She'd never tried to dismantle his barricade to satisfy her curiosity or to make a point. He'd even returned to the spot on his own while the orchard was being harvested last fall so he'd know there were people close by without having to make an issue of it, and he'd found the barricade still exactly as he'd left it. Mostly he'd checked to prove to himself that nothing had seriously tried to come out from the door in all that time, but it was also comforting to see that Adalva hadn't done anything to undermine him.

There could be no question by now that Adalva had settled very comfortably into a surrogate mother role to Jordan and Jane. She'd even helped Jane make gingerbread for the solstice feast and helped Jordan stay mostly clear of the aroma.

There had been no hint they should expect another stepmother. Father had always been a bit chagrined about the friction that had arisen between Eva and his children, and now that they were older, he seemed ready to let a favored friend of his beloved Calista indulge herself in bringing them up. No one was complaining. Even the usually wagging tongues of the kingdom's self-appointed arbiters of propriety seemed disinclined to suggest the baron might need a proper fourth wife.

Adalva could never be that fourth wife even though father got on with her as well as any woman, because priestesses didn't marry. If they had their own children—and they tended not to—they wouldn't have a father at all but would be the children of the goddess, Seriena. Jordan didn't understand how that bit worked, but, you know: religion, magic. If it made clear sense it'd just be stuff that happened and nothing mystical at all.

Adalva's story was near its conclusion now. He'd heard this one a dozen times, but he'd been listening to the old stories with a new appreciation the last couple of years.

"'How did you come by my son's sword?' the queen demanded, and Bryann replied, 'He must have dropped it after the fight, for I found it lying in the clearing on the ground. I came to return it and express my gratitude.' The queen's face wore a mix of confusion, sorrow, and doubt as she said, 'I thank you for the return of his sword, but I laid my son in the ground two years past.'"

The younger children in the audience *oohed* and *aahed* appreciatively, looking to each other with wide eyes. The older listeners already knew this traditional ghost story and quietly enjoyed the familiar telling.

One young gentlewoman toward the back, though, just a little Jordan's senior, was listening with an expression of haunted credulity that kept drawing his eyes back and back to her. No stranger to him, her name was Venah Montacute. It annoyed her. More than once he'd seen her stamp her foot in frustration and deliver the lecture that her family name meant "steep hill". She always followed up with an unflattering appraisal of the intellect of whoever had sparked the lecture.

The name fit her well enough, though, by his appraisal. Speaking as someone who was starting to understand what the big deal was about girls, he liked her look. It was what was going on behind her eyes right now, though, that really interested him.

"Now back to the feast hall," Adalva said, shooing her listeners toward the door before Jordan could follow up on that thought. "Young Lady Jane has a surprise for you."

Jordan already knew this would be Jane's gingerbread castle and he hung back, ostensibly to play the good host, but he'd already come up with a great many excuses to stay as far away from the aroma of gingerbread today as possible—and he wasn't about to stop now. His acquired revulsion to the holiday treat was putting a bit of a damper on things. At least he knew that Adalva would make excuses for him if necessary.

When the parlor had emptied out, Jordan closed the door and pulled out the book he'd stuck on the shelf here for just such emergencies. One of the best bits of the last two years was that he'd become Adalva's covert research assistant. Young lords weren't supposed to be scholars any more than they were supposed to be craftsmen, and Adalva's interest in all things weird was—well—slightly illicit in its own right, because she was more focused on describing the what than on explaining how it all came about, either because of the greatness of Seriena or the foul workings of demons. So while they didn't work terribly hard at concealing their activities, gathering more and more stories to share, they did make a point of not drawing attention to it.

As he combed through Adalva's little library and the new acquisitions he'd helped her find, Jordan kept a special eye out for any references to gingerbread. To date, he'd found just one about some old lady building a full-sized cottage in the forest out of the stuff. It got his hopes up for all of five minutes that it might be the clue he'd been looking for, but if the story related to his experience in any way, he couldn't see how or what details of it might help.

Perhaps it would someday prove a piece of a larger puzzle. In the meantime, the book in front of him dealt with the legend of a deadly demon who stalked battlefields and lonesome wilds in the form of an enormous black hunting cat. Again, not relevant, but it was interesting—and for now that would do.

The door creaked and Jordan quickly closed the book, forcing himself at the last moment to close it on a finger to hold his place so that maybe he could pass off his vague sense of guilt as a casual gesture. It was Venah coming back. At first she didn't see him there, intent as she was on watching the room behind her. She had slipped in and was starting to close the door when she finally spotted him, and she flushed. "I'm sorry, milord. I didn't mean to disturb your solitude."

It was the perfect opening, and he botched it. He was still trying to figure out what he wanted to ask her before he realized she was nearly gone again, and he simply blurted out, "Wait!"

"Milord?" she asked hesitantly, but she paused midway through closing the door behind her again.

He waved a hand uselessly for a moment, trying to pull words from the air before finally managing to turn it into a beckoning gesture. "It's okay to be here. I...just don't like gingerbread. Weird, huh?"

Venah gave a little shrug. "It doesn't do anything for me either. And...my mother, she won't touch honey. I don't understand it. Anyway, I just thought this would be a good moment to get some space."

They remained staring awkwardly at each other for a few seconds after she'd trailed off while Jordan considered and rejected several ways to ask her the question he wanted to ask. All of them made him sound crazy, even in his own head.

Finally, feeling she was about to bolt again, he opted for not asking a question at all. "I used to like gingerbread. A lot." He inclined his head toward a seat by the fireplace, hoping she'd take it as an invitation to join him. "But there was...an incident. Now the smell's all muddled up in my head with bad memories, so I stay away."

"An incident?" Venah asked, accepting the seat. She seemed content with the excuse not to return to the crowd.

"It was very...very strange. Maybe a bad dream instead of a memory. The sort of nightmare you never quite seem to shake." Finally seeing a way forward, he asked, "Does that make any sense?"

"Oh," Venah said, biting her lip introspectively. "Yeah. I think so. I guess I've had those."

Again there was silence. Jordan wished Adalva was here. She was good at this sort of thing—asking the delicate questions, putting people at ease. But she wasn't here. It was up to him. So how did she do it? He took a deep breath and closed his eyes, searching for the essence of Adalva in his life. Their conversations danced through his memory, picking up a sort of rhythm as he relived the most striking of them over and over in rapid succession: one, two, three, four, one, two three, four.

And there it was. Adalva never talked with you. She danced with you.

"You came to the old manor before it burned down, didn't you?" Jordan asked. "In my nightmare, I was out there in the middle of the night..."

So it began. Jordan knew he was no great dancer, but like anyone, he could feel the music, move to it. When it was particularly good he could feel it right down in his bones. Also when it was particularly good, he stopped thinking about it and just moved. Though Venah was doing nothing out of the ordinary, he could feel a music now in her words, in her gestures, in her eyes. He stopped thinking about coaxing her to say anything in particular and started steering her with gentle nudges as though she was his dance partner and he had his hand on her waist.

Safe behind the cover of the nightmare story, he told her about the whole incident in fits and starts, leaving her room to tell whatever stories of her own it brought to mind. All the while he scanned the rhythm of her reactions, searching her, reading her, dancing with her. He found himself deep in what Adalva would probably have called a "meditative state of mind" he might never achieve again but desperately hoped he would. It was intoxicating.

Within minutes the girl he'd barely known was a close friend and confidant as they shared details of their darkest nightmares with each other. After half an hour, there was no illusion between them that they were talking about literal nightmares. The word had just become their personal code for the things they'd lived through and feared sharing lest they be taken for crazy.

Venah shared her nightmare in fits and starts also, but it went something like this:

"There's an abandoned chapel with a graveyard in the wood not far from our manor. So, so many ghost stories about it. Still sacred ground, though, so nobody disturbs it. Most people stay well away from it, especially after dark.

"I used to love it, though. It was peaceful. Whenever I got my hands on a new book to read and could sneak away, that's where I'd go. Once, after my older sister died and I just couldn't take another moment of people, I even ran off and spent the night there, curled up by the old altar. There were the usual noises in the night, but nothing odd enough to get through my 'who cares'. And I had some disturbing dreams, but the kind I'm sure I brought in with me. It was just a night alone in my sanctuary.

"Then last summer, I had my nightmare. I was there later than I'd meant to be. I got all caught up in reading. Then I realized the sun was going down, but I was so close to finishing I lingered trying to. I've got like two pages left, racing the sun as it goes red behind the trees, when all of a sudden I hear this big splash and a boy starts screaming.

"There's an old cistern there behind the chapel that's been boarded up as long as I know, but the boards are old and the screams are echoing, so I figure they rotted through when I wasn't paying attention, the rains filled it up, and some fool's come poking around now and managed to fall in.

"I follow the ruckus around the chapel, and sure enough, there's the open cistern. Only—and I didn't think about this right away—the rotting boards had been torn up and tossed aside, not carelessly collapsed inward. Anyway, I'm edging up, trying to see down into the hole without taking any risks myself, when...

"Okay, you've got to guess this part. Seriously. No? Even you aren't going to believe me. Especially you aren't going to believe me. I'm dead serious, though.

"Out of the hole like a blast from a holiday oven comes the smell of hot gingerbread. Yes, really. If you hadn't told me yours first, I'd think you were having me on.

"Anyway, you remember that rotter Finlay Inglethorne? I know, don't speak ill of the dead, but you know he was a total rotter. I saw you two go at each other once. So this is Finlay down there and he's terrified, screaming for help and about how he can't swim. But there's like a twenty-foot drop straight down to the water with nothing but crumbling brickwork—and me with nothing on me but a book. Yeah, he didn't drown, he got thrown from a horse, but wait.

"So, rotter or not, at that moment all I was seeing was a terrified kid a little younger than us, and his screams are awful, so I run off and find a fallen branch I hope can float with his weight on it. I manage to get back before he goes down the last time, I toss it to him, yell I'm getting help, and just take off fast as I can because I can't bear the thought of being there when maybe it doesn't work.

"The nearest people I know are a farm family that live just outside the wood, so I run there and they grab ropes and half of them come with me, but I just know we're too late as we get near because the screaming's stopped. Then I think, well, maybe it worked and he's just floating there with his throat screamed raw, so I work up the courage to go up and look. Either he's floating or all I'll see is the water, right? Only I don't. I don't see him. I don't see the water. There's barely a puddle at the bottom.

"I am so grateful I didn't get all the way back to the manor for help. I know the farmers wanted to yell at me for my cruel joke, but they didn't dare. If it had been my parents instead, they'd still be making me pay for it.

"I really didn't know what to think, other than I might be going crazy. When I found out they'd put Finlay in the ground the week before, after the horse threw him, I freaked out all over again. I don't go to the old chapel anymore, of course. And I haven't dared tell anyone about it 'til now."

Venah gave a little smile of gratitude as the last of the story came pouring out.

Given the common threads in their stories, Jordan very nearly asked her if she was having him on, but the dance hadn't ended, and he could still feel the music. He not only knew she was dead serious about every detail, he knew she was terrified he might doubt her, just as he'd been terrified Adalva would doubt him, so he choked back the reflexive question.

Instead he found himself saying, "In the stories, it's nearly always the ghost of a complete stranger, isn't it? And if they're in trouble, they're reliving their actual death. I'm not thinking of a single other story where someone comes back only to die differently."

Venah, who sat slouched with her arms folded across her chest, lowered her chin to gnaw contemplatively at her wrist for a moment. "I can't think of one, either."

"You know this means we're not crazy, right?" Jordan asked.

Venah shrugged. "Or else really, really crazy. But yeah. And the weirdest bits are too much alike for our nightmares not to be connected. There's something very strange and very bad going on in our corner of the world."

"Adalva will want to hear your nightmare, too," Jordan said. "It's okay. She already knows mine."

"Thank you, milord." Her smile was warm and deep and sincere.

"Please don't ever call me that again. Whatever we're in, we're in it together and I need that. I'm Jordan."

Venah stumbled a bit over dropping the formality, but only a bit. "Thank you, Jordan. You know, a tiny bit of me wants to run off and beg your father to let me marry you on the spot just so I finally won't have to be alone tonight. I still hear Finlay screaming and pleading more nights than not."

Jordan chuckled sympathetically. "Not alone sounds nice. I don't even share a room with my pesky little sister anymore. Never thought I'd miss that."

"Be nice to pesky little sisters," Venah said. "They're probably just trying to tell you they love you the best they know how."

"Yeah. I guess." He smiled gently, not entirely convinced but ready to give the benefit of the doubt right now to anything Venah had to say. "I know you said you don't go there anymore, but will you show me where your nightmare happened when I can make up an excuse to visit?"

"I think I can do that," Venah said. "I'll show you mine if you show me yours."

And that, the song told Jordan at the quirk of Venah's mouth, was what flirtation looked like. As heir apparent to a barony, he'd already been subjected to several young women throwing themselves at him clumsily, but this was something different. This was a joke that was not a joke that had been layered over with an armor of, "Don't read anything into this." It was an invitation to extend an invitation to extend an invitation to think about considering possibilities.

The steps of the dance suddenly came rushing at him too quickly to keep up. He'd reached the point where he could no longer read her because she wasn't even an open book to herself. To avoid stepping on Venah's feet as the music came to an abrupt halt, he stumbled his way into a smile and a laugh. It was the emotional equivalent of rolling out of a fall.

Even before Jordan's own laugh had faded, he found himself mourning the loss of...whatever that had been. Still, he'd come away with the certain knowledge he'd found a genuine friend. Those had been in short supply since father had married up.

"There's still enough light to go look now," he said, "and it'll probably be months before we get another chance. Did you want to slip out before we get dragged back into the party?"

Without delay they made good their escape out onto the manor grounds, and no one who saw them leave was of a status to question what a young lord and his lady friend might be up to. The air was crisp and winter-cold—not bitterly so, but enough that they were grateful they'd managed to grab their good winter cloaks on the way out.

As they trudged through the snowy orchard they found themselves talking about anything but what where they were headed and what they were doing. Jordan brought up his lessons in swordsmanship, thinking it would be a good way to reassure her they weren't going out unprotected, but realized it wasn't going over well and that he hadn't brought a sword in any case. Still, once the thought was in his head, he sought out a sturdy tree branch of a good size and heft for beating back random assailants. He pretended he just felt like having a walking stick but managed to convince neither of them.

They walked on for a bit in silence with Jordan aware Venah was uncomfortable and not saying something, but otherwise found her thoughts distressingly opaque once again. Had he said something wrong? Done something wrong? The more he worried, the more self-conscious and awkward he felt and the harder she became to read. Finally the weight of it became too much, and he simply sat down in the snow halfway through the orchard.

"We don't have to go," Venah said. "I understand."

That would be for the best. Yes. If he'd already alienated his new ally somehow, he couldn't face the ruin anyway. They could turn around now and go back to the party and pretend like none of this had ever happened. Tomorrow she'd go home with her family, and on those rare holidays their paths would cross they'd be formal and polite, and they'd never again speak of nightmares. And he would be more alone than ever.

Slowly, Jordan got back to his feet, not making eye contact.

"Jordan?" Venah prompted nervously. "Wherever you've gone, please come back. Or take me with you. Just please don't leave me here."

"What?" he asked, confused.

"We're in this together, right? You said we're in this together."

"I...Yes," he said at last. And because the music had stopped and words no longer seemed adequate, he held out his open hand to her.

After a heartbeat's hesitation that seemed to go on forever, she took it with a whispered, "Thank you," and they finished the trek through the orchard with hands clasped, in silence. As they stood before the blackened ruin capped with snow, Venah broke the silence. "Some priestesses learn how to fight, you know."

"They do?" Jordan asked, feeling again that he had missed something.

"Yes," Venah said, still staring at the ruin while holding tight to his hand. "I have a cousin in the Inquisition. They have to be ready to fight demons and witches and heretics. Maybe even all at once. She showed me her swords. They're etched with holy symbols."

"Do you think she'd help us here?" Jordan asked.

"I haven't seen her in years," Venah said noncommittally, then added, "If we're in this together, will you teach me how to fight? My family won't."

Jordan didn't need the rhythm of the dance to know the answer to this one. "Yes," he said, losing the stammer and the hesitation. She squeezed his hand gratefully.

Maybe his low birth aided with the clarity. There'd been no professionally trained warriors in the world he'd been born into, but on the few occasions he'd seen a fight break out it hadn't mattered who was holding the axe or the pitchfork. People just tried desperately to avoid its business end. And while his memories of those days were hazy at best, they'd left him with the vague impression that what women lacked in size and muscle they made up for in sheer ruthlessness. Fighting fair was a luxury left to people who already had the upper hand. After all, those were the people who benefited from avoiding a sudden shift in the odds.

"Lesson one," he said, shoving the crude staff into Venah's hand. "If anything comes charging at you, whack it as hard as you can." They exchanged grins, then he released her hand long enough to track down a new club for himself.

Conveniently, Venah turned out to be left-handed, so they were able to push forward with their makeshift weapons at the ready while still holding hands. Nothing charged at them. Jordan hadn't really expected otherwise—but then he'd never expected to encounter his dead stepmother bricked up inside a wall and begging to be let out, either, so he was disinclined to take chances.

"So...that's the door?" Venah asked, staring at it as if trying to decide whether it might bite—which is probably exactly what she was trying to decide.

"Yeah," Jordan said. "Do we open it?" He was amazed he'd even asked the question. Until the moment he did, he'd always just assumed he'd try to keep it sealed forever.

Venah sucked on her lower lip, then shook her head. She stepped up close enough to poke the door with the end of her stick and gave it a tentative rap, poised to jump back and run. When nothing happened she tried again, giving it two solid thumps. Still nothing. She stepped back slowly and carefully, still not taking her eyes off the door.

"It has been a couple of years," Jordan said, despite the fact that he was having to remind himself to breathe as he waited for the door to begin shuddering from within.

"I don't smell anything," Venah said. "Do you smell anything?"

"Nothing I shouldn't," Jordan said.

"If we did open it, either we'd find an empty closet or we'd find something horrible, right?"

"Pretty sure," he agreed.

"Let's just come back together sometimes and see if we can smell gingerbread or if anything stirs when we knock. If we hide a cache of real weapons and such in the ruin, we'll be prepared to decide right then if it's worth the risk of opening the door."

It didn't escape Jordan for a moment that the plan included a commitment that Venah would be visiting with some frequency. It didn't escape him, either, that he liked that part quite a bit. He liked it enough that he'd have agreed to a far less sensible overall plan to get just that part. "Yes," he nodded. "Let's do that."

They retraced their steps back to the manor, still holding hands, though the desperation for reassurance had been replaced with a simple contentment with the companionability of it. The contentment lasted until about the time they were passing the workshop. Then it ended in a sudden shriek and a burst of white as Venah pulled away from Jordan, clutching at her face.

Jane's giddy laughter reached Jordan's ears a heartbeat before the second snowball burst harmlessly against his defensively raised arm. "Hey, sillies, you're missing the cookies!" She shouted from behind a snowy hedge.

"Jane!" Jordan shouted back. "You hit her in the face! You know better!"

"It was an accident!" Jane answered defensively. "I wasn't trying to."

"Yeah, well you did it anyway." Jordan scowled. When he turned to check on Venah, he found her on her knees in the snow, whimpering, with her face still buried in her hands. "Venah? Are you all right?"

"No!" Venah wailed, following up the exclamation with a string of epithets. "It hurts! I can't open my eye! What did she hit me with?" The tears were rolling freely down her cheeks.

"Snowball," Jane muttered, hanging her head and dragging her feet contritely as she emerged from around the hedge. "It was just a snowball. I'm sorry. I brought cookies." She bit her lip as she held forth a pair of gingerbread figures still lightly dusted with the snow she'd set them down in while preparing her ambush.

"That wasn't snow!" Venah screamed, finally lowering her hands. Both they and her face were caked with snow, but it wasn't pure. It was studded with traces of gravel, small chunks of ice, and crimson drops of blood.

"Go get Adalva," Jordan snarled at Jane. "Now! You are in so much trouble. Where did you even get that from?"

"I just scooped it off the ground!" Jane stammered.

"You dig in the snow, not the dirt! You know that! Go!"

Jane dropped the cookies and fled. Jordan slammed the heel of his boot down on one of them, shattering it and grinding the pieces into a packed mess with the snow. Letting out a shaky breath and trying to compose himself, he turned back to Venah. "Where did it cut you?" he asked.

"I don't know," Venah whimpered. "I still can't open my eye. I can't see. What...what is this?" She held up a shaky hand and winced as she tried to brush away the snow.

Jordan caught her gently by the wrist and managed to dislodge most of the snow from her hand by blowing on it. Blood swelling up from the tip of her middle finger instantly drew his eye to the little snarl of old wire protruding from it— some random bit of debris that had strayed from the workshop.

"Hold still," he warned her. The wire came out easily enough. It had slid in sideways and shallow when she'd clutched at her face. He also found a series of jagged scratches on her cheek, disturbingly near her eye. She still couldn't open the eye itself so he couldn't tell how badly it had been injured. There was enough blood around her eyelid to cause concern, but not enough to be terrifying.

Jane returned with Adalva in tow before Jordan had Venah halfway to the house, and the priestess immediately took over, guiding the girl out of the cold while she began questioning her about the injury. Jordan let them go but laid a restraining hand on his sister's shoulder before she could slip inside after them.

"What?" Jane demanded indignantly in answer to his scowl. "It was an accident. I said I was sorry, and I did like you said."

"Why did you want to hurt her?" Jordan demanded, managing to keep his voice even only by locking down his emotions hard.

"Accident?" Jane prodded. "You're not slow."

"Maybe the face was an accident," Jordan said, "but you're not slow either. All this snow lying around, and you root right down to the ground instead of scooping an easy handful off the top? And don't tell me you didn't notice the ice while you were packing it."

Jane's face hardened. "Accident," she insisted.

"Yeah, well you'd better hope she doesn't 'accidentally' lose that eye," Jordan answered coldly, "because you just broke father's hospitality. Don't think I'm going to lie about it for you." He let it drop and left Jane standing as he stalked back inside, looking to catch up with Adalva and Venah.

CHAPTER FOUR

SIEGE OF THE SANCTUARY

They wound up back in the front parlor, where Venah could sit in the good light from a window while Adalva examined her and cleaned the scratches. "It doesn't look too bad," Adalva said, "other than allowing it was a pretty savage snowball. I can't say I've ever seen one draw blood before. Go ahead and close your other eye, too. Good. Now can you pry the hurt eye open long enough to see how many fingers I'm holding up?"

Venah managed it. "None?" she hazarded, a bit uncertainly.

"Perfect," Adalva said. "You're going to have a lovely bruise, but as long as we keep the scratches clean you're going to be fine. Now we'd better go talk to everybody's parents."

She helped Venah to her feet and beckoned Jordan to come along. He caught her looking around for Jane, but she didn't seem concerned about not seeing her, so he just followed Adalva and they headed off. "You know," Adalva said to Venah, "if you want to keep that eye closed in style for a while I've got just the thing. In my odds and ends I have an eye-patch that belonged to Blackwater Molly herself."

"Really?" Venah said. "I never heard she'd lost an eye."

"I don't think she did," Adalva said. "Maybe it's just a pirate fashion thing. Or maybe it's some sort of magic talisman. Wouldn't that be amazing?"

As Jordan's concerns waned, so did his anger, and he began to really think about Jane. He still believed what he'd said about her doing this on purpose. The question was, "Why?" Surely he could get inside his own sister's head the way he'd gotten inside a near stranger's, even if he was already trying to think of Venah as an old friend.

His first thought was that this was completely unlike Jane, but that wasn't entirely true. It was completely unlike what most people thought of as Jane.

Guessing how most people thought of her wasn't hard. It was the story that got told over and over and over—a moment trapped in amber that would never be forgotten. It had cemented her reputation as a little faerie tale princess by virtue of being in the right place at the right time.

Early in the spring when Jane was 4, she'd been playing in the garden in front of the chapel and a beautiful rose-pink butterfly came flitting around her head. She'd reached for it. It had landed on her outstretched finger. She was still studying it in fascination when, unnoticed by her, two more just like it landed in her hair.

After that, they showed up in ones and twos, then fives and tens. After the first few, they arrived in all manner of sizes and colors, and soon Jane was laughing and spinning in the middle of a swirling cloud of rainbow wings. No one else even tried to crowd in. It was like a spell they'd all been afraid of breaking. It lasted for five minutes, maybe ten, then the cloud of butterflies dispersed as quickly as it had come until one lone pink butterfly sat perched on Jane's nose while she looked at it cross-eyed. Then it too flitted away and the butterfly garden remained completely butterfly-less for days after.

To the world at large, the Jane of that moment had simply been who Jane was ever since. Only it wasn't really who Jane was. At least it wasn't all she was.

No child is actually an angel, and there's no one better positioned to see that than a sibling. Siblings get front row seats to all the pettiness, the greed, the deception, the vindictiveness, and every other sin that might crop up.

In the case of those first two, Jane wasn't bad at all, but when it suited her she was at least as quick to lie as her brother was. The girl could certainly nurse a grudge, too, and wasn't above giving back worse than she'd got.

In Jane world, maybe this had simply been what passed as fair payback to someone who'd snubbed her cookies. Or maybe it had been a 'back off from my brother' message to someone trespassing on her status as his traditional partner in crime. Maybe it had been both.

Neither of them had ever had much in the way of friends outside each other. They got a lot of snubs from the other nobility in the kingdom over their father's—and Jordan's— lowly birth, and generally got too much deference from the children of father's vassals. It might be prudent for him to take Jane on some sort of adventure soon to reassure her she wasn't being replaced just because he'd finally hit it off with someone outside their little family.

As expected, Jordan's father questioned him about what happened, and as he'd promised, Jordan didn't lie for Jane— though he limited himself to describing the physical details of the snowball and left the adults to draw their own conclusions. Then he was dismissed.

He paused at the doorway, looking to Venah with a compulsion to still offer his support. When he caught her eye, she gave him a little smile and broke away from the proceedings to thank him for his help, then she added quietly that she'd be all right and she'd see him at the evening feast.

With a nod of acknowledgment, Jordan took his leave while their fathers hashed out what constituted justice for a little girl's minor violation of hospitality. As the baby of the house and the daughter of the beloved baroness, Jane could get away with quite a lot, but no matter how Father doted on her, there was no escaping the political equation on this one.

A lord who didn't deliver justice for his own vassals wouldn't remain a lord for long, and all his vassals were here right now under his roof to see how he handled it. Jordan's best guess was it would come down to a public scolding for his sister, followed by being turned over to Adalva to perform some sort of penance—just enough consequence to show that Father was taking the matter seriously. The scolding would doubtless sting Jane's pride, but she was clearly due.

Jane had apparently been tracked down by one of father's men. He was escorting her in as Jordan made his way out. She hit him with an accusing glare. He just rolled his eyes, shook his head, and kept moving. That look meant that, one way or another, drama was about to ensue. He was happy to be out of it.

Jordan returned to the party and made an attempt at being a good host, but found his thoughts still agitated, the noise too noisy, and the crowd too crowding. Besides, the scent of gingerbread still lingered everywhere.

Without consciously deciding to slip away, he found himself back outside, wading through the snow of the butterfly garden on his way to the chapel. There would be the traditional vigil there that evening as the sun set before the longest night of the year, but for the moment the sanctuary was soothingly deserted.

He kicked the snow off his boots at the door, then began the climb to the sacristia. He had his own key now. Ostensibly he was assisting Adalva in managing the ceremonial items stored there, but she'd really offered to share her sanctuary to help him heal and to work with her on building up the little library of odd tales. He set about that now, deciding he'd really come here all along to write down Venah's tale while it was fresh in his mind. Pulling out the journal he'd started, he curled up in the window seat and set to work.

Even fresh, it was more work writing down her story than it had been writing down his. His story remained etched in his memory even two years gone. Venah's was just a slippery collection of words and his imaginings they'd spawned. After crossing out a couple of false starts, he dug out some loose sheets of paper for writing a first draft on so his thoughts would be composed before he tried committing anything further to the journal.

The party forgotten, he let time slip away and had Venah's story half-added to the journal—her name diligently shortened to a nearly anonymous "V"—when he realized that the light from the window was starting to dim. Soon the party would be coming to join him in the chapel before adjourning back to the great hall for the feast.

From the scent of it, the early arrivals were already here, bearing pre-feast confections. Jordan began to wonder if the associations with gingerbread would ever let him truly enjoy winter solstice again. Then he heard the sob.

Jordan's immediate thought was, *Not again.* His next thought, after the initial moment of panic had passed, was, *Of course not again.* Someone was crying, yes, but that was all. He was in the safest place in the world—by far the holiest place he had ever set foot—with a crowd of worshipers already on its way, not in some lonely, abandoned ruin. There was still light to see by and candles aplenty. This was not ghost territory. He'd been primed to connect the sound to Eva by all the ways today had put those memories in the front of his mind. It was just a woman crying.

The only question was: did she most need his help or her privacy? Whoever it was must have come up here to get away from the crowds just as he had. Then another thought crossed his mind and he realized there were actually two questions. What if it was Venah?

She wouldn't have brought the gingerbread, but she could easily be crying because she'd been trying to get away from it and now it had followed her here, especially if the inquiry with his sister had turned rough. This had been no less an emotionally charged day for her than it had for him. He'd promised Venah he had her back. As long as there was any chance it was her crying, privacy would have to be a secondary concern, no matter how tempting it was to not get involved.

He stole up quietly to the door of the sacristia and listened, making a last attempt to figure out who it was before intruding on her. Whoever it was, she was no further away than the choir loft. For maybe half a minute he listened while the crying continued, but it remained too soft for him to say with confidence who it might be. Still, he hesitated with his hand on the door. It wouldn't be Eva. It couldn't be Eva. It well might be Venah.

He considered just calling out, but it seemed kind of stupid under the circumstances. He was only considering it because he was afraid it was Eva. But if he called out and it was Eva, that would be even worse. Open the door? No, he could wait it out. But Venah...

Was the smell of gingerbread actually getting stronger? Why was the scent so fresh, so warm, after making its way here through the winter air? He was being stupid. He was being paranoid. He was letting fear control his mind and rule his senses.

He couldn't breathe. He rushed back to the dormer window, threw it open, and leaned out into the crisp winter air, gasping for breath. His head swam. He collapsed into the seat and waited for the world to stop spinning.

The gingerbread smell hadn't gone away, but at least it was less oppressive by the open window. He should just lie here and wait for Adalva to come looking for him. That would only set him back two years. Well, maybe more than two years. At least two years ago he'd found the courage to batter down a wall under more forbidding circumstances. All he had to do now was throw a latch, open a door, step out into the choir loft...

Why wasn't being brave just a one-time-and-done decision? Was there ever a point where you could just fight down your demons and never see them come back?

He braced himself against the window frame as he leaned out again, gulping down fresh air. He consciously overlaid the nightmare visions in his head with an image of an overwhelmed friend come looking for space and quiet after a trying day, only to be overwhelmed by an abundance of Jane's baking.

Venah needed him. It had to be her, and she had to need him because that was the only reality in which he opened that door right now. Jordan drew a last deep breath. He held it as he returned to the door.

The door opened effortlessly. Beyond it, there was no sign of Venah. There was no sign of the choir loft or the landing or the stairs. Beyond the door—the door he'd come in by and the only door out of the room—lay nothing but a little closet with walls of gray stone. The closet was maybe three feet deep and no more than six feet wide, even counting the empty shelves on either side. Dark stains that might have been long-dried blood marred the floor.

The whimpering woman curled up with her back in a corner and her face buried between her knees had Eva's dark hair, had Eva's size and build, and wore a tattered, filthy, faded dress that could conceivably once have been one of Eva's favorites. Her skin was too dark to be Eva's, but that was the only reason for Jordan to doubt he was looking at his stepmother—other, of course, than the fact that Eva was dead.

He wanted to speak, to reach out to her, to comfort her. He wanted to slam the door and climb out the window onto the roof. What he actually did was freeze in shock and indecision, his hand still on the door handle.

Whether it was a moment later or minutes later he couldn't possibly say, but he remained frozen until the woman lifted her head, revealing not the dark face he'd expected, but a mottled mix of fair and golden brown. On the left side of her face, ghostly pale skin dominated, while the right side was predominantly dark. The same held true for what he could see of her arms, though the fingers of both hands were all fully brown. That detail jumped out at him in the middle of everything, because the image of the fingers clawing at the crack in the door still burned brightly in his mind, and they had been fair like Eva's.

The mottling of her skin was itself only mildly disconcerting, but the fair portion was covered liberally with scrapes, cuts, and bruises that never touched the darker portion. Even beyond that, the darker portion was artificially smooth, like a china doll or an expert wood carving or—well—gingerbread. That latter thought was sparked in part by the smell, of course, but also by the fact that her features there seemed almost painted on in unnaturally bright colors.

The right side of her mouth quirked into a fixed, macabre half-smile. Her right eye stared, blank and unseeing. Her left eye was badly bruised and nearly swollen shut, but it seemed to orient on him—if not focus—and the face contorted into a lopsided scream.

Jordan slammed the door. He leaned into it fumbling with the key and finally managing to lock it as the scream went on and on and on. He upended shelves to serve as barricades. He piled anything close at hand with even a bit of weight to it in front of the door. Then he clamped his hands tightly over his ears and rushed back to the window seat, still waiting for the scream to die away.

With his eyes on the door he perched ready for flight—to jump out the window, though he couldn't figure how he would find a way to the ground from there. On and on, the scream continued impossibly long as the door began to rattle. Then it stopped with the abruptness of a candle flame being snuffed and the world fell into deafening silence.

Jordan became aware that he had stopped breathing. He was about to draw a cautious breath when he felt the impact. Something had struck him on the back of the head, just behind the ear. Letting out an involuntary yelp, he instinctively rolled away from the impact and wound up on the floor, facing the open window that had been behind him. There was nothing there.

He lay gasping for breath, searching his senses, gathering his wits, until he'd finally recovered enough to realize the cold around his ear and the scattering of white powder on the floor meant he'd been hit with a snowball. Nearly in tears, he pulled himself laboriously back up into the window seat and yelled out into the gathering dusk. "That wasn't funny, Jane!" Only Jane was nowhere to be seen.

There was no one there at all. There was no manor. There wasn't even a roof. There was just a cemetery, forlorn and untended, blanketed in snow and lengthening shadows, so close beneath the window it barely counted as more than a step down into it.

Jordan's already-frozen heart cracked. Here was his longed-for escape route, but it neither looked nor felt like an escape. Was it better to remain trapped in an unbearable, sinister situation or to dash blindly away into a new and unknown sinister situation? Did his choices even matter anymore if the rules of the world he'd known had ceased to exist? Had he simply gone mad?

In the end he could think of only one way to answer any of those questions. He rolled out of the window, fully prepared to hit the slippery snow of the roof and tumble off to his death, but he only sank a few inches into the snow and then his feet landed firm and level.

He straightened cautiously from his landing crouch and looked around. Behind him there was still a chapel—but not Hollygrove chapel. It was an old thing and much less artistic than the one at Hollygrove. Tumbled down and long abandoned, it was in the process of being reclaimed by the surrounding wood along with its grounds and graveyard.

The window he must have come through was there, but it wasn't the sacristia he could see on the other side. It just peered into the interior of the ruin.

This time Jordan couldn't muster any sort of surprise. He'd actually been half expecting it. But what now? Even if he pretended he had nothing to fear from haunts out here—a pretense which he sincerely doubted—he hadn't come dressed for a winter night alone in the forest with nothing but a cold stone windbreak for shelter. He couldn't have even half an hour of light left, and he had no idea which direction would lead him back to a friendly hearth—or how long it would take to get there.

He was still miserably contemplating that cruel reality when a gingerbread cookie landed in the snow beside him. It was in the shape of a crude human figure in a dress with one leg missing—snapped off, by the look of it. With a sense of foreboding, Jordan slowly tilted his head back to look upward to where the cookie would have come from.

"Hey," Jane said, her affectation subdued and unreadable. She was sitting about fifteen feet up in an empty window frame that might once have held stained glass.

"Should I ask what you're doing here?" Jordan said, "Or should I ask what I'm doing here?"

"You should eat," Jane said. "You've gotta be hungry. Sorry. The broken one is all I had with me."

"No. Thanks," Jordan said.

"You made a real mess of things back home," Jane said, though her voice still contained no trace of stress or sadness or condemnation or, well...anything. She used to get that way sometimes, when she was very small, but she'd largely grown out of it. Somehow it was more disturbing than when she'd get angry.

"I made a mess of things?" he asked incredulously.

"Yeah," she nodded. "It's really, really bad. You'd better not come home. I'll help you run away, though, when I finish cleaning up your mess."

"Jane, you're not making sense," Jordan said. "Not even a little."

Jane shrugged. "Don't you know?" she asked. "The people with the power don't have to make sense. They just make the rules. Run away, Jordan. It's...odd. I'm really, really mad at you but I don't want you to get hurt. Run away. It's not safe to come home."

"You did this to me?!" Jordan demanded. "You brought me here?!" There seemed to be tears staining his cheeks. He didn't know if they'd been put there by frustration, sorrow, confusion, or some mix of the three. They were all vying for control of his body. Frustration seemed to gain the upper hand long enough to scoop up a fistful of snow and hurl it at Jane, but his aim was worthless and it exploded into powder against the wall well below the window and off to the side.

"The Montacutes live over there," Jane said, unperturbed, and pointed off through the wood. "I think you can get there before the light's gone. It'll be just the servants, of course, but they don't know what you've done yet and they'll put you up for the night. I'll get you stuff to help you run away in the morning."

"What have I done?" he asked with bitter sarcasm.

"You got people killed. Just go before it gets dark," Jane said. Behind her, a steamy fog came roiling upward. Backlit by flickering red firelight, it filled the window in a matter of seconds, though there was no trace of it from any of the other windows.

"Who are you? What are you?" Jordan demanded. "What have you done with my sister?"

"I don't know," Jane glowered. "Why don't you go wrestle another bear? Maybe it'll tell you." She rolled her eyes. "I could still change my mind about hurting you. Don't make it tempting."

Jordan could hear a cacophony of screams echoing out of the window along with the steam and the fire light. Was he staring at a portal into the actual underworld?

Jane didn't leave him long to ponder. She just shook her head, pointed the direction she had before, and said, "Go," one last time before rolling back off her perch and disappearing into the fog without a trace. Then the fog was gone as quickly as it had come, leaving nothing to see through the high window but a view of the same darkening sky that hung directly above him.

CHAPTER FIVE

Painful Decisions

None of this made sense. None of it. Still, he felt certain that he'd be dead before morning if he stayed where he was and saw no reason for Jane—or whoever might be masquerading as her—to trick him with false directions to shelter after bringing him here. Besides, the cooling steam had begun to settle around him and it smelled distressingly of hot gingerbread.

Primed to jump at every shadow behind every gravestone and every tree, Jordan fled headlong into the wood. Amid all the doubts and emotional turmoil, there was little room left for conscious thought in his brain as he ran, but when something did bubble to the surface it always came out as some variation on the theme of, "This is not good."

Running through the snow wasn't like running on solid ground. It might even have been stretching a point to call it running, but he hurried ungracefully as quickly as he could, his leg muscles burning from unaccustomed strains while his lungs burned from the cold air.

The one comfort was that it didn't take much light to pick out the difference between white snow and gray tree trunks, and he eventually managed to break out into the open again without once colliding with anything. He even had enough light left to make out the silhouette of the manor house ahead and orient on it before allowing himself to more slowly and carefully trudge the rest of the distance in the dark. After the difficult run, he felt every step as he climbed toward the manor, and it became increasingly easy to believe that Montacute did indeed mean "steep hill".

At last arriving at the stair to the main doors, Jordan took two weary steps up them before stopping himself and looking around. Most of the windows were dark, but a warm light spilled out from the ground floor—the domain of the servants—along with raucous singing to the accompaniment of pipe and tambourine. With the lord's family gone for the holiday, the household servants were holding a solstice celebration of their own. They'd likely still have someone posted to keep an eye on the front door to avoid unpleasant surprises, but...

Jordan found that he'd sat down on the step and begun crying in earnest, though the emotion behind it was no less muddled than it had been behind his initial tears at the old graveyard. At least the run had warmed him up and he wasn't shivering at the moment. That was good because he couldn't go inside. Not yet. He did his best thinking when he was alone, and he desperately needed to think.

Adalva always said it was no good trying to solve a big problem all at once. You had to isolate one little problem at a time and work each through until the big answers started to emerge on their own.

So what were the little problems? The first one had been the prospect of surviving through the night. He seemed to have that one nearly handled, so time to tackle another one.

Was that really Jane he'd been talking to? It was hard to be sure of anything when he'd clearly stepped out of a window at Hollygrove and landed within running distance of Montacute.

Well, he was certain of that, wasn't he? So Jane or...No. He needed to stop wasting energy on wishful thinking. She'd been plain enough with her jibe about the bear. And if it had been some sort of malevolent spirit, what would the point have been in making him this twisted offer of mercy? He didn't want it to be Jane but he had to accept that it had been until some actual evidence to the contrary came up.

So, his sister could...what? Steal doorways? Reroute one threshold so it connected to another? There was magic in thresholds. That had come up a lot in reading his way through Adalva's little library of the weird. There was magic in doorways and windows, in streams and in fences, in dawn and dusk and in the turning of the seasons. But when had she learned to channel that? How had she learned to channel that? And why did it smell like gingerbread?

With the sun gone, his thoughts were already starting to lose focus in the deepening cold, but he cudgeled his brain into working a bit longer. If he accepted the "bear" comment as proof he really was dealing with Jane, that meant he'd always been dealing with Jane. The hot gingerbread smell that had come pouring out of her portal today had come pouring out of her portal two years ago. Did that mean his own sister had been responsible for entombing their stepmother alive?

The least complicated answer was, "Yes," and Adalva had always stressed the importance of starting from the least complicated explanation and disproving it before moving on. That had never seemed more important than now, when the number of sane options approached zero while the number of insane options seemed infinite. So the working story was Jane could rearrange thresholds, the woman in the closet was whatever remained of their stepmother, and Jane had put her there. Was that even plausible? Was she even emotionally capable of something like that—assuming she was physically capable?

Jordan wanted to say "no". Maybe yesterday he would have gotten away with saying it and left it at that. But he couldn't deny the petty viciousness of that snow-ish ball she'd hit Venah with, nor the memories it had stirred up of how vindictive Jane could be. And the girl who'd thrown that snowball had been learning to master her impulses for two years longer than the girl Eva had backhanded to the floor just before her funeral. If that younger girl really had the power to entomb Eva, would she have even tried to resist the impulse?

At last the music started up again in Jordan's head, only it wasn't with the gentle give and take of his dance with Venah. This tune was the dark and dangerous story of power run amok where it didn't belong. Without Jane there to fill in the missing notes for him, he knew the tune was incomplete, but still he knew what he did know.

This really was his sister he was dealing with, mistress of her own magic. She'd been grateful enough to him for standing up for her with Eva but not satisfied with his relatively feeble tricks. She'd done it—she'd entombed Eva—telling herself she'd come back and let Eva out once she'd learned her lesson, but then she got to thinking letting Eva out would endanger her secret and be an invitation to land herself in a whole lot of trouble. From there it had been a small leap to telling herself Eva deserved it anyway.

Power corrupts. That was another of Adalva's favorite sayings. Wherever Jane's magic came from, it was too much power that she'd come into too quickly and too early in life. In light of their stepmother's fate at her hands, it was making excuses to simply think of his sister as vindictive. Jane had become cruel. She'd become murderously cruel.

Had Jane crossed a line from which there was no return? He didn't want to believe that. He didn't know if he could believe that. Annoying or vindictive or cruel, she was the only sister he had. She was probably the only sister he'd ever have.

He was old enough now that even if he did get another sister, it wouldn't be remotely the same. She wouldn't be someone he grew up with, a natural-born ally in discovering and dealing with the world. On top of that, he'd promised Calista he'd protect her; and father would be heartbroken just to learn what Jordan had figured out here, thinking things through in the cold.

Speaking of cold, though his mind was still nagging at him and there were threads of the tune that still teased just at the edge of hearing, unresolved, Jordan had reached the point where he could no longer ignore the elements. He got up, dusted off the snow, wiped away his tears, and finished the climb to the manor's entrance.

The Montacutes' servants fussed over him for a while, but once they were assured the heir to the barony was whole and well and comfortable—so that none of them were at risk of being held responsible that he was not—they were happy enough to leave him sitting uncrowded in a chair by the fire with a bowl of stew to finish his contemplations.

No further profound insights were forthcoming for him, though. The music floating up from below, less muffled than it had been outside, worked at cross-purposes with the music in his head. So did the sounds of general merriment. The earlier sense of certainty now eluded him. Even the pieces he'd already puzzled together he might never be able to share. Well, he sort of had to share it with Venah, provided he ever saw her again. They'd agreed they were in this together. But not even Adalva would be ready to hear what he had to say about Jane. Maybe not even if he had more to gone on than, "It's the only way to make sense of all the pieces."

So where did that leave him? Back with the choice between going home and running away. Seduced by power or no, he still trusted Jane to lend him aid with the running away bit, and if she could change out where any door opened to, that would be a lot of help.

That was serious sorceress-league magic like hardly anyone claimed to have ever seen, much less been able to wield. And if he defied her? How strong would the bonds of blood be then? This wasn't just a matter of vexing a kid sister anymore. She'd already proved he was at her mercy. Would he have any protections left from her murderous cruelty if he angered her now? Of course, if he didn't face her now, he'd be at her mercy for the rest of...

No. Jordan slammed down that line of thought cold. Facing his fears two years ago hadn't been the wrong choice, but a fear of fear could no longer serve as his north star when every choice left involved facing down fear on multiple fronts. There were no right, smart choices he could make from where he suddenly found himself.

No matter what he did he was in for a world of hurt and so were a lot of other people, several of whom he loved. Jane had claimed people were already dying because of him. He doubted her casting of the blame but not the claims about death. Who had already died? How? Why? The questions kept coming and coming and coming, but this time no answers came with them.

Did he even want to know what the real story was? If he ran away from home now, he could make up any story he liked. He could tell himself it was someone annoying or dreadful that he barely knew, patch things up with Jane, and maybe even go on a grand adventure with her, seeing the entire world. But then what if it really had been someone despicably dreadful and he disappointed Father and Adalva over unfounded fears and he left Venah to deal with all this alone right after promising he had her back. But what if...His mind resumed chasing around in circles.

All right, then, he decided. If there were no smart answers and any decision that didn't get him killed was likely to leave him miserable and haunted enough to wish it had, it was time to re-frame the question.

Sooner or later, everyone got plunged into an abyss of troubles from which they could never emerge. Being the son of a baron meant he was being raised to be ready to take to the battlefield if the need ever arose. Warriors had been facing this same basic dilemma since time immemorial. How did they cope when all the choices left to them looked like different forms of suicide?

Looking around, Jordan found himself alone save for the old porter slumped on a stool in a corner near the front door. He straightened up when he noticed Jordan's scrutiny. Jordan gave the man a wan smile, set aside the cooling, half-eaten bowl of stew, and walked over to the porter.

"Milord?" The man straightened further.

"Did you draw the short straw to be away from the party?" Jordan asked.

The porter shook his head. "Volunteered. I've seen my share of parties and wouldn't rob the young ones of their turn."

"What's your name?"

"Donovan, milord," the man answered.

"Were you ever in battle?" Jordan asked him earnestly.

"Aye." Donovan nodded. "A couple of times."

"Did you ever feel certain you were marching off to die?"

The porter's eyebrow raised just enough to betray his doubts that this was a casual question. "Not as such. There were times I had to wonder, yes, but I can't say I ever felt certain."

"Have you ever known a soldier who felt that way?" Jordan asked. "I know it happens. How does a body cope with something like that?"

"I don't suppose anyone knows how they'll deal with something like that until they're actually there," Donovan said with a hint of shrug, "but I thinks it comes down to choosing who you want to be. If you can't choose not to die, you choose how to die, 'cause that will be the final word on who you were and how you lived. You write your own epitaph, as it were, an' hope it makes it onto a grave marker for you. That's my best guess, anyway."

"Do you think it helps?" Jordan asked.

"Everyone who really knows is dead, milord," Donovan said. "But, yes. I think it maybe helps just a little. I think it can at least keep a body moving long enough to maybe save someone else, and that's no bad epitaph." He paused for a few beats, studying Jordan. "May I ask who you're going to war with?"

"Only if you don't expect an answer." Jordan sighed. "A big part of my problem is there's no sane way to explain my problem. Thank you for your thoughts, though."

"Must be a mighty big problem if it brings you here alone, now of all times, without even a horse and without being properly bundled."

"Aaaaand you folks have already sent someone to check with my father about what's up, haven't you?" Jordan sighed.

"Of course, milord." Donovan gave a good-natured little laugh. "The master of the house has to answer to your father, not you, and you've not been recognized as a man grown just yet. The Montacutes would have our hides if we let anythin' happen to the baron's only son. That makes your morbid turn more than a bit worrying."

Jordan drew another sigh, long and deep. "It's not a literal choice of deaths," he said after a long pause. "Just no good options."

"That's...comforting," the porter replied.

"You're right, though," Jordan went on. "If there's no solution to my problems, I can still choose to solve someone else's. I need to get back to Holly Grove, and I need to get back there tonight, not in the morning. I need a horse."

"Lord or not, you'll not be leaving here alone in the dark," Donovan said evenly.

"I was tricked into coming here," Jordan said. "Because of the particulars, I'm afraid your young mistress, Venah, is in danger. I have to go."

"All the more reason I need to go with you," Donovan said firmly.

Jordan started to open his mouth, but closed it before the sentence could spill out. The insights were coming easier already. If he tried to dissuade a proud combat veteran by telling him this was dangerous, he'd only insult the man and entrench his determination. Instead of letting the words out, Jordan just nodded and bit his lip as he rephrased the thought.

"Your company would be welcome, but come ready for danger and trust no one—no one—no matter how harmless they appear. There's treachery afoot tonight and I wouldn't rule out black magic. If you've an eye-of-Seriena talisman to watch over you, please wear it, if only to humor me."

Humoring Jordan seemed an apt description of Donovan's behavior as they rode out from the manor, reasonably bundled against the cold and on better horses than Jordan thought he'd had a right to hope for. The man worked hard at keeping a stream of light-hearted chatter going in a transparent attempt to lift Jordan's spirits, but the farther they went the more frequent his pauses became and the longer they lasted until

Jordan could tell the old man was becoming concerned despite himself.

Finally, in response to a querying stare, Donovan admitted to the thought that was nagging at him. "We should have passed Benedikt on his way back from Hollygrove by now, whether he was makin' the return alone or in company. We'll hope things aren't so bad as your worries, but somethin' isn't full right."

Following the rutted road by lantern light, they set no speed records—but at least they did have the one fresh set of hoof prints in the snow to follow, so there was no concern for straying off the path. That allowed them to make a little better time, and the silhouette of Hollygrove broke the starry backdrop of the sky well before the long night was half over.

"Well, ye've gone an' made me paranoid and no mistake." Donovan sighed as they drew closer.

"So you're wondering where the party is too?" Jordan asked. There were no lights—not so much as a thin sliver flickering beneath a door or out from a shuttered window. There was no music. There was no laughter. There were no sounds beyond the muffled tread of their horses' hooves in the snow and the light jingling of the harnesses.

Even if the general celebrating had broken up by now, it was traditional to keep a fire going all night on the winter solstice to greet the dawn. With some trepidation and still clutching the lanterns they'd brought for the ride, they climbed the stairs to the front doors. They'd barely started before the gingerbread scent hit.

"At least they've kept the ovens busy," Donovan said, drawing a deep breath of what was to him an enticing aroma.

Jordan had known this moment was inevitable, if not when it would hit. Choking down an impulse to panic, he instead marched resolutely up the stairs and reached for the handle of the great doors, hesitating only a moment before pushing them inward.

Warm air hit him like a blast from an oven. Whatever lay beyond the doors now, it wasn't his home. It looked like some sort of cave, but with roughly worked walls and reinforcing timbers. All lay in darkness save for what lantern light they'd brought with them.

The frown that had never left Donovan's face deepened. "Is it supposed to look like this, milord?" he said, perplexed.

"Close enough," Jordan said. "Would you keep an eye on the horses while I see where everyone's got to?"

"I'll feel better about keeping an eye on you 'til we see where everyone's got to," Donovan said.

Jordan let out a little sigh. He'd tried. "Come on then," he said, beckoning. "But by 'close enough' I meant that it's a space enclosed with walls and a ceiling. Everything else is entirely wrong. This would be some of that black magic."

Donovan snorted but otherwise said nothing as he stepped up beside Jordan and began looking around as well. He moved to close the doors, but Jordan cleared his throat. "I don't see anything good coming from closing ourselves in here. Do you?"

"I can't say I do," Donovan admitted, aborting the effort.

"Any chance you'll believe me now if I say I got to the woods outside Montacute by climbing out a window in the chapel here?" Jordan asked.

"I might at that," Donovan agreed.

"And that there was no sane way to tell you what was wrong?"

"That's seeming more and more a fact, milord."

"Good," Jordan said. "Let's build on that. And when I said trust absolutely no one, I meant be extremely suspicious of my sister. You'll probably be able to spot her. Little noblewoman, not yet 10. Looks like me. She's mixed up in whatever's going on and she's taken a real dislike to Venah."

"Thank you for the warning," Donovan said. "Anything else I should know?"

"That the last thing my sister said to me tonight was that people were dying here," Jordan said. "Other than that, no. The rest is less believable."

"And here I'd thought all my adventures in life were behind me." Donovan chuckled darkly.

"You can still go if you like," Jordan said.

"Why would I?" Donovan asked. "To go sit by the fire a few more years, telling stories of how I walked off an' left the young heir to the barony at the mercy of black magic 'cause it was giving me the willies? Think I'll write me some other epitaph, thanks."

It was Jordan's turn to snort. "I'd say you've got more than a few years for sitting by the fire."

"Mayhap," Donovan shrugged. "Mayhap not. But if you think telling that story for a lot of years sounds more fun than telling it for just a few, you truly have gone mad, milord. I'll be stayin' close, thank you very much."

It didn't take them long to explore the crude, near-featureless chamber and find a single tunnel leading away, and it didn't take too many paces down that before they came across a crude message scrawled in charcoal on the pale stone wall. "Run away," Jordan read aloud for the benefit of Donovan, whose questioning look he took as a hint of illiteracy. Without further comment, Jordan just shook his head and moved on with the lantern held high. That decision had already been made.

They passed similar messages two more times. The cramped tunnel twisted and turned, following either the shape of the original, natural cave or a vein of some mineral chased by miners. If it either climbed or descended, the slope was too gradual to say for sure, but the heat and the smell of the spices slowly intensified as they went.

A fourth message declared, "You always were thick." Jordan didn't bother to read that out loud, letting Donovan assume it was just more of the same. Then a fifth message declared, "It just gets worse." On the floor beneath the message lay the complete skeleton of some animal Jordan couldn't identify with certainty. It might have been a dog or a wolf.

"Jane!" Jordan shouted down the tunnel, his scowl deepening. "I'm not leaving without answers!" The only reply was his own voice echoing back to him. They kept going.

The tunnel opened out on the right side, where a natural cleft about three feet across and several times as long cut a chimney up and down through the rock. In both directions it vanished into darkness, but the heat and the aroma rose straight up out of it from below. Jordan and Donovan kept close to the solid wall on their left as they made their way carefully past. Beyond it, the air finally began to cool and freshen.

"Last chance," the sixth message announced. "You don't want to see this."

Ahead, the tunnel opened back into the snowy night. They found themselves stepping out into the butterfly garden through the archway of an arbor. A lone figure lay slumped in the shadows at the foot of Calista's statue.

They drew closer, Jordan's stomach knotting with the certainty that it would be Venah, but this time his instincts betrayed him. He hadn't been pessimistic enough. It was his father. It was Jane's father. It was *their* father. The good and caring man who'd sired and raised them both lay broken before the monument to his great love, Jane's own mother.

Taking in the scene with a level of horror Jordan had thought he'd gotten past, he could see a bloody trail in the snow where the baron had been dragged. He had fallen not far away, from what must have been a high window in the manor house, and he'd not landed well. His body was a mess, and that's all Jordan's mind could take in before it shut down and his eyes closed. The next thing he was aware of he was on his knees in the snow with his back to what remained of his father, fighting down waves of nausea and dizziness.

"My arm is yours, Lord Jordan," Donovan said quietly behind him. "What would you have me do?"

The sentiment snapped Jordan's mind back into focus. Was Jane's motivation as simple and cynical as all that? As women ruled the spiritual world, so men ruled the world of secular politics or father would have been simply holding the barony in trust for Calista's daughter. As things stood, Jordan and not Jane had just inherited the barony—but if he had run away as she'd urged, this would all be hers now.

Had she already arranged for him to take the blame for father's death somehow when he suddenly disappeared? Could his own sister truly be that...awful? Well, she'd been awful enough to commit patricide. It was all but certain their father's death was her doing. He must have simply stepped over the wrong threshold without looking where he was going. If she'd really killed their father that way, would she hesitate to do the same for him?

"I would have you watch your step," Jordan said at last to Donovan. "Don't trust any door. Don't trust any window. Don't trust any arch. And now I'd better tell you why." But even before he could get started, he was interrupted by a cacophony of tortured shrieks that rolled abruptly out from the chapel doors as they swung slowly open.

If the window behind Jane back at the ruin had opened a portal into the underworld, now Jordan found himself staring at its front gate. Again, steam came pouring out, obscuring a horde of shambling figures backlit by a fiery glow. Donovan's fingers traced a protective circle around his heart in the sign of the sacred mirror before the man eased a small axe off of his belt and stepped between Jordan and the approaching crowd.

CHAPTER SIX

HELL IS A BAKERY

Slowly, the indistinct shapes began to resolve into the silhouettes of men, women, children, and even animals. Donovan shouted a challenge but found his voice drowned out by the screaming. He started urging Jordan back the way they'd come.

Jordan thought better of it and pointed out across the grounds. Stepping through a door right now might not be the last thing he wanted to do, but it was more than close enough for conversational purposes.

Speech was useless. Coherent thought proved all but impossible. Donovan just nodded his acknowledgment to Jordan's gesture, and they ran. With no apparent option but retreat, they headed around the house for the horses, risking the occasional glance back as they went.

At first, it seemed the shambling figures would simply be left behind, but by ones and twos, some of them began to peel away from the crowd and pursue more quickly. Jordan caught sight of a great dark mastiff that had broken out ahead of the pack in a lope. It let out a discordant howl as it picked up speed, then they were around the corner of the manor house and it disappeared from view.

"They aren't there," Jane's voice called from above. She was leaning out a window on the next floor up. "I let your horses go."

"Jane, what are you doing?" Jordan demanded. "What have you done?"

"I'm trying to clean up your mess," Jane said dryly, "but you keep making things worse."

While they were talking, Donovan backed up against the wall of the manor and waited at the corner for the mastiff to catch up. It met his axe as it rounded the corner and it went down with a yelp.

"Yeah. That's not gonna help either." Jane sighed, looking down at the bloody mess in the snow. In the time it took Jordan's gaze to flicker from the fallen mastiff to Jane and then follow her gaze back to the mastiff, the thing was already lurching unsteadily back to its feet despite its fractured skull.

Donovan jumped back, cursing, and turned an accusing glare up at Jane. "You are a witch," he growled.

"Witch?" Jane laughed mirthlessly and shook her head. "I'm like one step down from goddess."

"Oh, sure." Jordan returned the laugh and added a biting edge to the lack of mirth. "That's why you're so careful to keep out of reach. You're a brat living on borrowed black magic."

"You know you actually have to die now too?" she responded calmly. "I'm sorry, Jordan. That even makes me a little sad."

There was no more time to talk, even with Donovan having stayed focused on hacking the mastiff's legs out from under it. More...things...were already appearing around the corner. Jordan and Donovan ran. Every few windows they passed under, Jane was already there waiting for them.

"You're wrong, too," she called down. "This isn't black magic. Why do you think Seriena doesn't mind me opening doors in the chapel?"

He tried to ignore her. He tried to shut out conscious thought. His emotions had mostly already gone numb from overuse. He could try again to make sense of things later. Right here, right now, there was only survival—survival and his sister, who was suddenly letting out a startled yelp as she came flying out the window. Somehow she maintained enough presence of mind to twist around, to protect her head and keep her limbs from striking the ground at odd angles, but she still landed hard in the snow from a drop of nearly twenty feet—and Venah landed half on top of her despite the twisting.

Venah rolled away, whimpering, clutching her arms together hard about her chest, though Jordan couldn't rightly tell whether she was reacting to pain in arm, chest, or both. "Kill her!" Venah made her best attempt yell, but it seemed all she could do to force the words out of her throat. "For go'ss sake kill her!"

Jordan hesitated. Donovan didn't. Jane screamed as he stepped between the two girls, raising his axe. She lifted one arm in a defensive gesture then she, Donovan, and Venah all disappeared under a thundering wave of water that came pouring out of the open window.

Jordan paused for a further moment, waiting for the torrent to pass, but it showed no sign of abating. A raging waterfall now poured out from the window of their home—melting the snow, gouging the earth, and spreading out in a widening pool—as if it intended to become a permanent fixture.

Jordan didn't stand still for long. He didn't dare. Instead, he ran around the widening edge of the pool, trying to catch sight of any of the three through the torrent. It didn't help matters that Donovan's lantern had been extinguished instantly. No doubt the glass had been shattered. Now he had nothing to see by but his own lantern and the meager offerings of the stars overhead. Even the moon was providing no help tonight.

It was Venah he found first. Coughing and spluttering and in obvious pain for it, but alive and crawling laboriously away from the torrent through mud and water that was surely so cold it must already be hungrily siphoning away her life's warmth. He set down the lantern, waded in himself to grab her arm, and set to dragging her clear with little care for the immediate pain it caused her.

All the while he kept scanning for any sign of the others. He was halfway back to the lantern when he spied them together, just clear of the torrent. Donovan was struggling up onto his hands and knees, apparently oblivious to Jane standing over him, his axe in both her hands and raised above her head.

Jordan didn't have time to do more than shout a wasted warning, his voice lost in the thunder of the waterfall. The axe came down sloppily, but with more force than it had a right to in the hands of a battered and disoriented 9-year-old girl. Glancing off Donovan's shoulder blade, it was still enough to drive the older man back down in the mud and draw a distressing amount of blood.

Desperately, Jordan dropped Venah back into the shallow water, but by the time he was clear of her, Jane had already landed a second blow and a third. The second had hit Donovan's skull, the third his neck, and the overall effect was to keep driving his face down into the mud where he'd be unable to draw a badly needed breath. By instinct, Jordan rushed to shove Jane off of him, but by instinct he also drew up short. The frantically swinging axe forced him to consider his approach, and in that moment he also realized the full weight of the choice he was about to make.

With no time to decide and only guesses with varying degrees of wildness to go on, he had to weigh the chances he could still save Donovan's life, the chances he could still save Venah's life, and the chances he could save anyone else who might still be in danger, lost within the maze Jane had turned their home into. He also found some part of him hadn't given up on surviving the night still himself. He even found a flickering little hope in there somewhere that he might somehow get his sister back—but that last one died at the look of sheer, manic ecstasy on the sodden girl's blood-spattered face as she readied another blow.

Jordan paused long enough in indecision and in horror at her expression that she landed the blow. It probably didn't kill Donovan, but it likely assured that he wouldn't survive the night. And whether it was making excuses for himself or not, the memory of Donovan's dedication to keeping both Jordan and Venah alive while writing his own life off as largely over ended the indecisiveness.

Donovan was lost. Jordan's sister was gone. His father was gone. And if the closest thing to a mother he had in the world was still alive to be saved, his best hope of finding her now lay shivering and vulnerable in the mud behind him in the body of the new friend whose back he had promised to protect. With dark shapes looming closer at the edge of the lantern light and Jane relentlessly raining down blow after blow with the axe, Jordan splashed back to Venah and forced her to her feet, not waiting to find out if her legs could take the weight.

In this one thing luck was with him. She staggered but she stood. Then he scooped up the lantern and they were running together haltingly, with Venah hurting and crying and shivering and unsteady but forcing herself to keep moving all the same. However the fall had hurt her, at least she'd escaped any glaringly obvious fractures.

There was no question of throwing any of the planning to Venah. Jordan had to free her up to focus on simply putting one foot in front of the next. "Whatever this is," he murmured, urging her on with a renewal of their earlier promise, "we're in it together." But their options were limited and dwindling fast. Whatever magic Jane was working, she could work it miles away. That meant no door or window within miles would be safe.

He could see by now that, as Jane had said, the horses weren't where they'd left them. Maybe, if the doors to the stables still opened into the stables, they could still find horses there. That made it their best option. It also made it their most obvious option, and Jane had been doing too good a job of anticipating his moves. To make things worse, the stables weren't particularly close, and he had to change the game right now while she was caught up in this mad blood lust that was consuming her. It was also safe to say that between the two of them, one would never see another night fall on Hollygrove Manor. He couldn't leave not knowing if he might have saved Adalva. Well, maybe the direct approach?

"There's no time for the whole story," he said, "but is Sister Adalva alive or dead?"

"I can't say she's dead," Venah panted. "Too many people are, but I think she lives. Your father—"

"I know," Jordan cut her off.

"My brother, too," she said. "A few people I barely knew. Mostly she's been dropping people one by one into the torments of the underworld. Does that count as alive or dead? But she sealed off the manor, so all the outside doors and windows just lead right back in somewhere else, and she's been hunting us."

Venah kept wincing in pain, though it was hard to tell how much was triggered by the effort of talking compared to the effort of simply moving. "She doesn't even have to be in the room. I caught her spying through a keyhole to see what was happening in rooms on the other side of the house. Change where a door leads at just the wrong moment and...She's mad, Jordan. She's mad and she's vicious and she meant what she said about killing you."

"Are you as cold as you look?" he asked.

"Pretty much, yeah," she admitted. "I'm not going to last long out here. You...You don't have to tell me."

"I've got to try to save Adalva," he said. "I have to. And anyone else I can get out. So either I run ahead to the stable and..."

"Don't go there," Venah scowled. "We're in this together, remember? And I've still got family in there too. We just need a ladder or something to get back up..."

"Wherever the window you came out of leads now, it's not back into the house," Jordan said. "We're not getting back in the house. But how deep are we into this together?" She seemed to have exhausted her current capacity for words, but she prompted him with a questioning expression. "Will you follow me into the abyss?" He nodded toward the front doors of the manor, still billowing clouds of steam out into the night. Venah grinned fiercely through the pain.

As best Jordan could tell in the dark, they'd momentarily lost all pursuit. Everything that was chasing them seemed to have stopped back at the new waterfall, whether in confusion or out of some eagerness to help or witness Jane at her bloody task. Regardless of the reason, it bought them precious time to get up the stairs and close the doors.

If luck held and their pursuers really hadn't witnessed that, they just might conclude he and Venah had simply doused the lantern and tried to lose themselves in the dark night. If. So he kept pushing Venah on through the blessed infernal heat until they'd lost themselves around a couple of bends and he dared to let her catch her breath and take stock of the damage.

"Here," he said. Stripping off the warm fur cloak that had come from her household, he passed it to her. Then he stripped off his tunic and pushed that at her, too. "I'll stand watch. Get out of those wet clothes and try to figure out how badly you're hurt. I don't think there's any way she can spy on us here, but..."

"I've got this," she nodded, urging him back toward the last corner they'd rounded with a game smile. "I snuck up on her once already, remember?"

They both had had some token training on treating injuries, but neither more than that. Venah's best guess was that she'd cracked a rib or two in the fall. Now that she wasn't breathing hard, rushing around, or trembling constantly, the pain had subsided a little. She was badly battered and bruised but seemed only slightly broken. She could manage okay with a walk. She wasn't looking forward to trying to run again.

"Next time, just shove her out the window," Jordan teased while she was dressing after the diagnosis. "No need to throw yourself out with her."

"I know she's your sister, Jordan, but I had one shot," Venah said soberly. "I still don't think I'll ever get another. I was honestly hoping to drive my elbow into her as we landed, maybe break her back or at least shatter a few ribs."

"She's not my sister," Jordan said, latching onto the anger in hopes it would overwhelm his grief—and in hopes it would steel him to dealing with the unthinkable. "Not anymore. Forgiving what she's done isn't even an option because, yes, she will kill me if I let her.

"I failed her mother. I failed our father. I failed her. How could I stand so close to her all her life and not see her turning into this monster?"

"We make excuses for the ones we love," Venah said. "We always do. I wasn't there, but I can't imagine you're at all to blame. Something's broken in her—deeply, profoundly broken. Can you recall anything in her life that might have broken her like this? Anything at all?"

"I..." Jordan hesitated, considering the question seriously. "No, I can't."

"Then forgive my sacrilege, but if you want to blame someone, blame Seriena. How many times have you been told she's everywhere watching over everyone? Right here on your own estate, her mirrored eyes look out from behind the altar of the most beautiful monument to her in the entire county. She saw what you couldn't see and still allowed this to happen. She even let Jane desecrate that monument by turning it into a gate to the underworld.

"I'm not going to ask you to turn your back on Seriena. I *am* going to demand you pick a fight with her before you go picking a fight with yourself." The little diatribe was punctuated throughout by little grunts and whimpers as she worked to find the least painful way to pull his tunic on.

"All right," she said at last. "I'm as decent as I'm going to get. Let's stop pointing fingers and salvage anything we can."

As they moved on, she caught him studying her bare legs. He caught her studying his bare chest. They exchanged sheepish grins, deciding it was a fair trade, and re-focused on survival.

When Jordan tried to lead the way, Venah protested. "Which of us here is the barony's reigning hide-and-seek champion?"

"Ummm...we have a hide-and-seek champion?" Jordan asked.

"As of about ten minutes ago, yeah," she said. "I just stole up behind a sorceress on her home turf. I've always loved hiding. I'm good at it. Plus, I'm not good for a lot else right now. Give me this. So long as we're playing a nice, slow game of hide-and-seek, I'll be our scout. Just point me the way."

The tunnel still opened out into the butterfly garden, and at that point he was grateful to have Venah leading the way. It allowed him to stay focused on her and not let his gaze wander to the base of Calista's statue to see if...anything had changed.

The roar of the waterfall could still be heard from around the side of the house, close enough still to mask any other sounds that might have been useful to overhear. The garden seemed to be deserted at this point, though. Probably everything that had come lurching out through the chapel doors earlier was away scouring the grounds for them.

The doors themselves still stood open, still loosing clouds of steam into the night, backlit by that red glow, and still issuing forth a chilling chorus of screams. Now that they'd made it this far, the thought of just taking Venah's hand and fleeing into the night suddenly took on a whole new appeal for Jordan. They'd actually have a chance now that she was warm and dry.

With the doors just a few paces away, they exchanged nervous glances and he could tell the same misgivings were running through her mind. He could lead her away. They could run and never look back, lose themselves in the wider world and start over together. There was no doubt she'd go with him.

Then the moment passed. Neither of them had asked it of the other. Jordan nodded toward the doors, she acknowledged silently, and they hurried together through the gates of hell.

Hell, it turned out, was a bakery. That is not to say it looked in any way innocuous, but they arrived through a free-standing arch that looked for all the world to be made of gingerbread and was glazed with odd, arcane symbols that screamed "witchcraft" to the untrained eye. It was also decorated with skulls embedded into the structure of the arch. There were canine skulls and feline skulls and rodent skulls and bird skulls and, right at the top where a keystone might have been, what looked like the skull of a single human infant.

The ground seemed to be paved with slabs of gingerbread, the slabs cemented together with white icing and outlined with femurs and other long bones. The gingerbread courtyard disappeared off into the roiling steam in all directions. There were no walls visible, just a scattering of freestanding doors and windows placed seemingly at random, all the doors closed, all the windows shuttered. Those windows weren't even set into walls. They just hung in the air as if daring gravity to say anything about it.

At least a dozen gibbets, also scattered at random, added to the disconcerting decor. Each of the suspended cages held some gaunt and disfigured shell of a person, glassy-eyed but still screaming and convulsing like they were suffering a sudden and violent death rather than a prolonged, languishing one.

In the middle of it all stood a huge brick oven with cast-iron doors nearly large enough to fit a gate house. The doors stood open, and the fire raging inside cast a hellish glow over the entire scene.

"Oh, go'ss." Venah was hyperventilating, staring at one of the cages. Judging by the remnants of their clothes, most of the captives had been peasants. Two or three might once have been merchants. This last, though, would have been a young lord—Finlay Inglethorne, to be precise, though it took Jordan more than a moment to recognize the emaciated creature.

Venah ran to see if she could open the cage, her face screwed up in an expression that combined terror, pity, and revulsion. "Are there keys?" she asked. "There have to be keys."

"That doesn't mean they have to be *here*," Jordan answered, trying his best to hit the necessary volume to be heard above the din without projecting hard enough to be heard very far. He grabbed Venah's hand and pulled her away. "Family first. Come back if we can."

Even as he said it, he felt no hope of that becoming an option, but he had to keep them both focused and moving. The captives here hadn't even acknowledged their presence. That might mean they were already beyond saving. More and more this was becoming an exercise in simply taking the edge off the worst of the damage.

"Then what do we do?" Venah pleaded, covering her ears for what little it was worth.

"We keep moving and we hope." This was where his plan had ended. He'd had no idea at all what to expect once they got here. "Check the doors. Peek through if you can. Keep each other in sight. And never, ever step through a door unless we're holding hands, okay?

"I was gone so long because she dumped me out a window miles away. We can't let her separate us again." Jordan managed to avoid saying the rest out loud, but he felt with dreadful certainty that if Jane were to separate them again it would be the death of them both.

Venah nodded, still spooked and wide-eyed, but ready to cling to the reminder of their united front like a woman drowning. It wasn't hard for him to understand the sudden cracks in her bravado. The sight of Finlay must have brought all the nightmares she'd been suffering for months back to her in a single rush.

They tried a couple of doors and found them locked with nothing visible through the keyhole but darkness. Through the keyhole of the third door they still saw nothing but could hear rushing water—perhaps the source of the manor's new waterfall.

Before they could try a fourth, Venah caught Jordan's attention and directed it over to a grate in the floor that had been too far away to make out through the steam when they came in. It was a circular grill that looked like it had been scavenged from somewhere to lay across a jagged hole punched in the gingerbread floor. The rusting metal of the grill had been inexpertly painted over in stripes of red and white, as from some childish attempt at festivity. More cries drifted up from below, but clashed with the tormented screams from the cages around them. These were a chorus of desperate cries for help.

Dropping down at the edge of the grate, Venah began to call out, but Jordan cut her short with a hand clapped gently but firmly over her mouth. "If you call loud enough for them to hear over all this, who else will hear?" he asked. She nodded and he removed his hand, but it was clear she was getting even more rattled by all this than he was—and that was saying a lot.

It wasn't just Jane they were in a race against time with now. How much more of this environment could they endure before going insane? He straightened up, offering Venah a hand, but she froze with eyes and mouth wide halfway through reaching for it. Jordan found himself trembling in dreadful anticipation as he turned to follow her gaze. At his shoulder, with her face not a full arm's length from his, stood the patchwork Eva.

CHAPTER SEVEN
DO YOU WANT TO KNOW A SECRET?

Jordan froze too as the woman studied him with an inscrutable expression and one poorly working eye. "Jordan?" she asked haltingly. The inhuman side of her mouth didn't seem to be working too well. "You're...big." At least that was his best guess at what she was saying. Her voice came soft and uncertain, barely audible above the screams. "Are you dead too?"

How odd, a detached part of Jordan's mind noted, that the woman who'd haunted his nightmares for the last two years suddenly seemed like the second-least worrying thing in his world. But that was all the thinking he had time or room left for. His capacity for planning and caution exhausted with this last start, he just grabbed both women by the hand and began dragging them bodily toward the door they'd come in by.

"Come on!" he goaded them. "Come on!" Within a few steps they'd broken into a run to keep up with him, and Venah was too preoccupied with relief at the thought of escaping to care how much pain she was in for it. Seconds later they burst out from the door and into the butterfly garden, crossing it in a rush and not even consciously hoping they hadn't been spotted until they were back in the tunnel with the door closed behind them. Even then, there was barely time for that thought before

Gingerdread

Venah slumped down to the floor, back against the wall, clutching at her chest.

"Are you—" Jordan began.

"Yes," Venah hissed through gritted teeth. "I think so."

He watched her in concern for a moment, but her pain seemed to be slowly ebbing—or at least not getting worse—so he left her to cope with it and turned his attention to the other woman. "Eva?" he asked.

"I...think so," she answered, her voice still uncertain as she studied her own hands.

"What happened to you?" he demanded bluntly.

"There was pain," she said. "It seemed like a lot at the time. Then I remember waking up in the small place. I screamed and screamed but no one heard me for the longest time—not until you showed up. I remember you tried to rescue me. Thank you for trying. Do I get to stop hurting now?"

"I...don't know," he said honestly. "I still don't understand what's happening. I think the more you can tell me the better chance I have of helping you." In her eyes he could see hesitancy, uncertainty, as she considered her next words.

"I know it's Jane's fault if you're worried about that," he reassured her. "And I'm not mad at you anymore for hitting her. You shouldn't have, but that's done and past and I just watched her kill a loyal man in cold blood. She's guilty of even worse, isn't she?"

Eva bit the fully human side of her lip and tears rolled down that cheek as she slowly nodded. "She's got monsters, Jordan. She's got monsters and she won't let me die." Eva seemed inclined to leave it at that but pushed on in answer to the prodding in his eyes. "I don't know where her witchcraft comes from, but she says it's divine power. Jane thinks she's the daughter of Seriena herself, never Calista of Hollygrove. She says Seriena made that chamber of horrors just for her."

87

"And do you believe that?" Jordan asked.

"I don't know what to believe anymore," Eva whispered.

"What can you tell us about her magic?" Venah asked, finally pulling herself up to sit properly. The worst of her pain seemed to have subsided. "What is she capable of?"

Eva seemed to ponder the question for many long seconds. "She opens and closes doors as she pleases," she finally said, "but sometimes it takes more out of her than others. It ebbs. It flows." She continued to speak soft and haltingly, dragging out every sentence. "I've never seen her do it so effortlessly as tonight."

"Maybe if we just survive long enough she'll get weaker again?" Venah floated the idea hopefully. "Have you seen a pattern?"

Eva shook her head. "I only see her when she's tormenting me. I'm mostly locked away. She could just get tired."

"But if it's not just getting tired," Jordan said, "if it's something special about tonight, that would fit. Doors and windows, the night when the days have stopped growing shorter and will start lengthening again, even the line between life and death she seems to be blurring...It's all threshold magic. All of it."

"Threshold magic?" Venah asked.

Jordan closed his eyes and held up a finger for silence as he fought to recall tidbits from the stories in Adalva's library. "She sent me out a door miles away, but so far I've only seen her open doors in caves and ruins and our own home—thresholds that either had no owner or that she had a right to. Have either of you ever seen her open a door into a place owned by someone else?" He opened his eyes again to find Venah shaking her head. Eva took longer pondering but eventually shook her head too.

"We need iron," he said quickly. "We have to get to father's workshop."

"I will go," Eva said. "The monsters ignore me when they have other jobs. They have other jobs tonight. I only have to stay away from Jane—and she could show up anywhere."

"Thank you," Jordan said. He reached out to touch her arm in what he intended as reassurance, but she flinched away, and he let the gesture go uncompleted. "We need hammers. We need nails. And do you think you could get to the stables, too?"

When he'd finished with his wish list, Eva headed off down the tunnel with one hand on the wall to guide her through the dark. "You have a real plan?" Venah asked with a certain amazement as they watched her go.

"Yeah," Jordan said. "But it involves a huge leap of faith. I've never gotten to try any of this stuff out."

"Still," Venah said, "that puts us way ahead of where we were ten minutes ago."

"Jane?" Jordan called into the night. "Jane?! I'm tired of running, Jane! Let's end this!" With the lantern in one hand and leaning on the spear in the other, he stood alone in the butterfly garden, standing over their father's body.

Eva had come through wonderfully. She hadn't been able to reach any armor for him, but she'd found both the spear and a sturdy, short sword. He'd be stretching a point to claim he was competent in the use of either, but at least they made him feel a little less naked and vulnerable to Jane's unnatural servitors.

While he waited for the response, he turned slow circles, peering into the darkness. "And if you want to know a secret, show up yourself! It'll be too late to do you any good if you think you can get it out of me later!" His voice didn't carry the bravado he'd been trying for. His throat was tight, his doubts were constricting his chest, and he kept having to blink back tears, but all that was at least partly his own fault.

He didn't want to be here, keeping company with the worldly reminder that his father was forever gone. Despite his talk of no longer having a sister, and despite the abstract understanding of what was at stake tonight, he feared his resolve would break if he didn't keep the tangible proof right there in front of him as to what needed to be done and why.

It seemed to take forever and might really have been only seconds before Jane's "monsters" began edging into the lamp light, surrounding him. He counted no less than ten—though he was more preoccupied with keeping an eye on them lest they charge than he was with getting an accurate head count. Some of them might still have passed for badly battered humans with glassy-eyed stares. There was no dog this time, but a mangy cat and one large bull with a hide entirely the color of gingerbread. Everything else seemed to be a patchwork creature like Eva had become.

Jordan was sizing up the circle, picking out the primary threats and the weak links, when Jane—now a blood-spattered mess—finally stepped out of the shadows beside the bull and laid her hand on its flank. He told himself that was a good sign. She was reassuring herself. Despite all the power at her command, she clearly remained cautious and scared. She could talk all she wanted about being a goddess, but she was still trying to convince herself as much as anybody.

"What's this big secret?" she asked without preamble.

"Only if you'll answer me some questions first. You owe me that much. We both know I won't be getting answers later." He cast his eyes meaningfully around at her monsters.

"I don't owe you anything," Jane answered coldly.

"Doesn't matter," he said. "It's the price of my secret. Yes, you'll find out eventually, one way or another, but like I said, not in time."

"All right," she assented finally. "Ask."

"How many people have you killed?" Jordan asked, trying to keep his voice business-like and neutral. Again, he didn't succeed terribly well.

"Here tonight?" Jane asked. "Or in all?"

"Let's start with tonight," he prompted.

Jane began a slow count of her fingers. "I started with Venah's big brother," she said as she ticked off the first. "If she's going to take you, then I get a fair trade. But Dame Riffingham saw, so I had to kill her, too." She ticked off the second finger. "Well, one of the scullery maids screamed—you know the one with the dimples—cause I guess she saw what I did to Riffingham." Jane ticked off a third finger. "That brought that guard with the droopy mustache and the one with the big ears." Fourth finger. Thumb. "After that, the whole house was in an uproar and I was having too much fun and I realized, hey, I can really get away with this."

"Tonight of all nights," Jordan said, trying hard to let his mind just skim the surface of her words without really thinking about them. "On the solstice, when the world of the dead collides with the world of the living."

"See?" Jane smiled. "You're not so stupid. Not smart enough, but not stupid."

"Who else?" Jordan asked grimly.

"Three more of the guests." She ticked off the fingers. "I don't think you know their names. I don't. Then there was Father." She ran out of fingers and started over on the original hand. "Another servant. Another guest. Then that guy you brought back from Montacute with you. I guess that's thirteen.

The last was the most fun—all up close with the blood everywhere. Is that what being drunk feels like?"

"You killed thirteen people?"

"Yes," Jane answered with a nod.

"Just tonight?"

"Yes. I've only ever killed two in a single night before and those were just peasants." She waved a hand dismissively.

"How many in all?" Jordan asked.

"Twenty-five I think." Jane shrugged, then looked thoughtful as she did some mental calculation. "Yes. Twenty-five."

"Why?"

"Like you could do better," she replied scornfully.

"Why any at all?" This time he couldn't suppress a glower.

"Because I got bored with the animals." She shrugged again, then laughed at his expression of baffled revulsion.

It dawned on Jordan at this moment that Jane really was in no hurry to kill him. She was experiencing the same sort of liberating relief he'd gotten from sharing his secrets with Adalva. Had she ever had anyone to tell them to before? Well, anyone who wasn't basically already dead?

He could work this, but it could also backfire. If she really did kill him, he wanted it to be quick, not lingering as her captive audience. Still, it might already be too late for him to back out. Best now to keep her talking.

"You said something about being a god?" he asked.

"Almost, yeah." Jane smirked. "Seriena's my real mom."

"And you know that because...?" Jordan prompted.

"Because she told me. She talks to me. I've actually seen her three times in the chapel mirror."

It took some effort not to challenge Jane on that. Coming face to face with Seriena was basically unheard of, even for the holiest of women. What she was describing sounded more like the trickery of a demon. If the chapel had never been consecrated properly—if it had been usurped by some unspeakable power from the underworld—that would explain so much. But he couldn't confront her with that. One glance down at their father reminded him that this wasn't about trying to persuade Jane or save her. Too much blood had been spilled, too many lines crossed, too many bridges burned.

"That's...incredible," Jordan finally settled on saying. "I can't imagine."

"I can't let you live, Jordan." She sighed. "No point making nice. I gave you a fair chance. I've played along. I've let you buy your little girlfriend a head start to run away. Now what's the big secret?"

"Okay." Jordan nodded. "You forgot about something. Do you hear that tapping?"

She cocked her head, listening. It was faint and distant, coming from the far side of the house, but she seemed to hear it and nodded warily.

"It's important. Can I show you?" He pointed to the door nearest the garden. When she hesitated, he rolled his eyes and added, "It's not like I can run anywhere you can't catch me. You can even hold my spear if you want." He lowered the spear and tossed it sideways in her direction. It landed in the snow near her feet. "I just wanted to make sure I wasn't going to get rushed by your friends before we could talk."

Jane finally acquiesced with a nod, and Jordan walked over to the door, unmolested by her creatures. He opened the door slowly, revealing the underground tunnel Jane had routed him through. "Just like you left it, right?" he said.

Surreptitiously, he glanced up above the door frame without tilting his head back to betray the motion. Yes. It was there. They hadn't dared secure it properly, so he'd been half-afraid it had already fallen and sunk into the snow. So this was the moment of truth. Had he guessed right or was he about to die screaming?

"That tapping, though," he went on, "that's the sound of doors closing to you. The secret is why they're closing. They're closing because you killed Father."

Jane scowled skeptically.

"I think you'll know why if you think about it," Jordan said. "And you'll know it's true. What happened when you killed Father?"

"What?" Jane demanded.

"The minute Father died," Jordan said levelly, "ownership of the manor—ownership of the entire barony—passed to me. It's mine now. And for killing Father and breaking his hospitality, I disown you, right here, right now. We are no longer kin, you are no longer in line to inherit, and Hollygrove is no longer your home."

He wasn't really sure if that threat about the inheritance would hold up, but if ever a time existed for bluffing, this was it. "You are now and forever an exile and an outlaw. Not a door in the entire barony will welcome you, not a cave or window is yours to claim. All of which means..." He pointed back toward the tunnel even as he glanced over his shoulder.

The tunnel was already gone, replaced by the little antechamber that normally lay beyond the door. It was all Jordan could do to keep from screaming, "Thank you, Adalva!"

"Kill him," Jane snarled, but Jordan was already through the door and he had slammed it shut behind him before any of her friends could get halfway to it. He threw the bar as something thudded into the door with a heavy crack. Without waiting to see how the door fared under the assault, Jordan scrambled away to the narrow stair that servants used to get from here to the level above and he hurried to the window looking back out onto the butterfly garden.

"You know what else?" he shouted down to Jane. "I deny you any right of dominion or ownership over any creature living or dead that has called this land home. You're free. All of you. Go to your rest!"

"Don't listen to him!" Jane screamed as her pack of minions paused, looking slowly back and forth between the siblings. "That's not how it works!"

"Yes it is!" Jordan bellowed, fervently hoping he had a clue what he was talking about. "Go!"

The cat was the first to come to some sort of decision. It threw itself at Jane's face with a horrendous screech. With a shriek of her own, Jane threw up her arms in time to have her forearms and not her face gouged by the clawing, hissing, bedraggled thing. Then, as abruptly as it had turned on her, the cat simply stopped moving and fell limply into the snow. One by one around her, the creatures began to collapse.

"No!" Jane shrieked. She threw her arms up toward the window where Jordan stood, in a gesture similar to the one that had loosed a waterfall earlier. Jordan recoiled instinctively even before the hellish light and intense blast of heat hit him. He was pretty sure she'd just opened the window straight into the brick oven in her chamber of horrors.

Well, that answered that. His pronouncement alone hadn't been enough to bar her access to all the portals in the barony—at least not during this night of the solstice. Without the added power of the iron horseshoes Venah had been gently tacking above the doors of the manor, he'd already be dead. No doubt now that if he did live through the night his first edict as baron would be to require a horseshoe be securely nailed above every door and window in the domain to protect its threshold from evil.

The heat from the oven was so intense that it drove Jordan scrambling back to the far side of the room. Then things got worse. The oven sparked and popped and hissed, belching flames like an extension of Jane's own anger. Embers landed on the carpet. The carpet began to smolder.

Jordan tried to ignore the heat and force his way closer so he could stamp out the embers, but it would be no use if he couldn't sever Jane's connection to the window. Like the waterfall, this presented an ongoing problem. In fact, it was probably the continued roar of the waterfall that had given away his bluff. However protected the doors might be, she still had power over the windows. Now she knew it. And that meant...

That meant he could no longer hear her screaming her outrage because she was retreating into her seat of power. She would either be sprinting back into her torture chamber, filled with doors that belonged exclusively to her, or—if that connection had been severed—she'd be in the chapel, hurrying up the stairs to where she could reach a window and enter her sanctum from there—and then what other horrors could she still unleash?

As the smoldering carpet burst into flame, Jordan gave up on fighting it. He gave up on the manor. He'd deprived Jane of her home; now she'd never let him keep his, and she still had all the power she needed to back up her hunger for revenge. For the second time in his young life, his home was about to burn. All that he could salvage—all he could let himself care about salvaging—was the people.

CHAPTER EIGHT

FLAME AND FLOOD

He rushed to the great hall, shouting the alarm, and was relieved to find Venah already overseeing what had been a quiet exodus out the front doors of the manor. That had been the second exit they'd secured with a horseshoe, and Venah would have taken Jane's first outraged screams as her cue to start trying to get people out through them.

He desperately wanted to make sure Adalva was okay, but if he started singling people out, that would remind Venah to look for her family—and if she didn't know her brother was dead already, this was not the moment for her to find out.

"Everyone, out out out out!" Jordan commanded. "The manor's on fire and we can't put it out. Everyone to my voice then out! Take any warmth, light, food, and weapons at hand, but forget everything else!"

He rushed up to Venah and lowered his voice. "Her monsters are gone and she's lost power over every protected opening, but the rest are still a danger. Get a fire started out on open ground and get everyone to gather at it." He went back to shouting hasty orders that delegated authority to Venah for handling the evacuees. There wasn't time to bring anyone else up to speed, and most everyone seemed shaken and disoriented. At least there seemed to be few injuries.

Grabbing the two nearest of his father's knights—his knights—Jordan announced they were going to look for stragglers, but that no one else was to follow. "Either you're with me or you're gathering outside where the fire is being built. Anyone off by themselves is still in danger."

Whatever they knew about what was going on seemed to be enough for them to take him seriously. They knew they'd been trapped by some sort of black magic. They knew people had been disappearing. They seemed to know one of those people had been his father and he seemed to be old enough now that no one questioned whether it was his place to step in and take charge. For the moment, that would do.

Rushing around a burning manor house searching for stragglers when every door, window, arch, or cabinet might suddenly turn into a deadly trap proved nerve-wracking, to say the least. He made a point not to pass through, or even pause directly in front of, any of them he didn't absolutely have to. Even calling into rooms instead of searching them, it was taking a long time. It was taking too long. If Jane wasn't watching his every move now, it could only be because she was too busy setting up some devastating surprise.

"Jordan?! Jordan?!" Venah called. They had reached the upper gallery by then, and he could see her down on the main floor of the great hall. "Have you found my brother? He's still missing!"

And there it was. Without even stopping to think, Jordan knew this was the moment Jane had been waiting for. It was her music stuck in his head now, if you could call that awful, ear-piercing discord music.

Killing people was nothing to her because she honestly didn't care whether they lived or died. She cared about their pain. She hungered for it. It satisfied her twisted soul as thoroughly as that first "dance" with Venah had filled his. That was why the barbed snowball. That was why Jane filled her sanctum with the screams of the damned. That was why she'd killed Venah's brother and not Venah. That was why she would kill Venah to get to him.

"Run!" he shouted, pointing forcefully to the door. Why had she come in so far? "Run!"

"That's it. We're done," Jordan told the men as he broke into a run himself. "Get out!"

He hadn't gone ten feet before the report of shattering glass announced the arrival of a new waterfall pouring in from the window directly above the main door. Then another window burst, then another, until a deafening deluge was roaring in through every window in the great hall.

From up in the gallery, Jordan could catch glimpses this time of the source of the waterfalls. Some seemed to be coming from pitch black caves, but mostly he spied bridges of brick, stone, or wood. Jane had to be capturing the flow of every river and stream for miles around.

The attack was at once better and worse than Jordan had anticipated. Safe to say, the great hall at least wouldn't burn now—and this was no precision trap. This was the last, desperate brute-force assault of a girl who knew her time was running out.

He'd already lost sight of Venah, though, and Jane could be using the sound and fury as cover for pretty much anything. His memory flashed to the sight of Donovan staggering back to his feet from under the force of that first torrent, replaying the bloody moments that followed, and he ran faster. If Jane was desperate and feeling pressed for time, she'd be falling back on what had worked so spectacularly well before and given her such a rush.

Out of the corner of his eye, Jordan caught a flicker from the archway he was passing just in time to throw himself down and roll forward. The sudden rush of water still soaked him through and slammed him hard into the gallery railing, but the man behind him didn't get so lucky. The force flipped him straight over the railing. The fall wasn't so far that it was a death sentence, but likely broken bones followed by a merciless pummeling from the torrent probably meant he wouldn't be getting out of the manor under his own power in any event.

On the assumption that Jane had spotted him from below, Jordan kept low and clawed his way out of the torrent, crawling along next to the wall. Then he forced himself to start thinking like Jane again. She'd know about where he was because Venah had pointed him out to her and she'd have worked out the route he'd be taking. She wouldn't be straining to see him through the chaos because she didn't have to.

Not waiting for the other knight to catch up with him, Jordan scrambled back to his feet and broke into a dead run. As the next arch loomed, rather than try to hurl himself past it, he veered abruptly to the side and hurled himself through it. He bounced off a wall, rolled through churning water, and came up on the main floor of the gallery facing Jane from ten feet away.

She had the axe with her, but thankfully slung at her side. The immediate problem was the spear he'd left her. It was currently lodged in Venah's rib cage, pinning her against the floor, trapped beneath a waterfall as she struggled to catch a breath.

As he watched Jane's expression melt from gleeful malice to panicked alarm at his sudden arrival, he knew she had only one play left to her, which meant he had only one play left to him. By the time he drew his sword this would all be over. Instead, he launched himself at her in a race to beat the deluge that the panicked Jane would be slamming into his back.

It hit him before he hit her, but it hit too late to stop him. He wrapped his arms tight around her as the water bore them away together and all he could do was pray that he'd just freed Venah from the spear instead of driving or twisting it into something vital.

Pinning a girl Jane's size should have been easy, but she fought him with more ferocity than she had any right to be able to muster. As the swirling waters tossed them about, he found himself struggling just to make sure she couldn't get a grip on either her axe or his sword.

When the waters slammed him into a support beam, he lost the struggle. She grabbed and drew his sword—but though the weapon was relatively small, it hadn't been designed for close-quarters grappling. Jordan knocked it away before she could bring it to bear, and the sword went swirling away into the icy tumult. He only realized grabbing his sword had been a sucker move when she used the distraction to plant a knee firmly in his groin. Before he knew it, she had squirmed out of his weakened grip and splashed away, fumbling to ready the axe.

Gritting his teeth, Jordan staggered to his feet and after Jane, trying to catch her before she could disappear completely into the deluge. Too late. She vanished behind a waterfall, and all he found on the other side was an arched alcove. She could be anywhere by now.

Unarmed and with his back to a wall, he cast around desperately for the site of her next ambush. What he found was the broken and half-drowned knight who'd gone over the railing. The man's sword remained hanging from his belt, safely tucked away in its scabbard. Jordan scrambled through the treacherous waters and grabbed for it, cursing his cold-numbed fingers.

He didn't have it half drawn before the axe slammed into his shoulder blade, eliciting a scream of pain and sending him tumbling headlong back down into the water. He barely managed to roll over in time to catch the next blow in his left forearm instead of his face. In addition to the deep cut it left, he was fairly sure she'd managed to break a bone.

As he struggled to right himself before she could swing again, a flash of hope sparked in Jordan when he finally caught sight of the other knight, sword out and splashing across the great hall behind Jane. Jane saw the spark in his eyes, though, and hurriedly slammed the axe down hard at his skull again, trying to get in one more blow before she had to deal with some other threat. As a small mercy, she still had the blade oriented wrong after retrieving it from his arm, and it was the back of the blade that slammed into his head like a hammer. He didn't quite lose consciousness, but the world did darken and go completely out of focus, like he was watching it through a distant haze.

He fell again and landed on his good arm. It propped him up just enough to keep his head above water for the moment, but his limbs had become largely unresponsive. Simply willing them to move was like trying to force his way through mud.

He watched as Jane spun to spot the oncoming knight, found she still had seconds to spare, and turned back to face Jordan. She didn't try to speak above the roar of the water, but she did level a single finger at him in a clear promise that she'd be making sure this was finished. Then a spear lanced out of the archway she'd ambushed him through, piercing her side.

The last thing Jordan saw was Venah twisting the spear. Then her face—contorted with pain and determination—was replaced with one more wall of water. He had a moment to think Jane, panicked and disoriented, must have shifted the threshold in the wrong direction because the wall of water hit them and not Venah. Then everything went fully black.

"Jordan? Jordan? I need you to wake up."

It was Adalva's voice, but they were the most profoundly stupid words he'd ever heard her say. Even mostly asleep, he could feel the pain pressing in. Sleep was what he needed. Lots and lots of sleep. She could wake him when he'd healed. Or not. Oblivion sounded pretty inviting right now.

She kept prodding him, though, gently but insistently. "Just wake up and drink this, then I'll let you sleep."

It slowly dawned on him that either he was already dead or Adalva had survived, so there was that. And as she showed no signs of giving up and letting him sleep, he eventually forced open his eyes a crack and mumbled, "M'wake."

It hurt every bit as much as he'd expected. His jaw hardly wanted to move at all. He'd yet to experience a hangover, but this felt akin to the worst complaints he'd heard about them. On the plus side, he seemed to be dry if not warm. He was wrapped in blankets, lying in a bed, and he could smell the wood smoke of a nearby fire even if he couldn't feel the heat.

"How many fingers am I holding up?" Adalva prodded.

"Stl nun," Jordan managed to her satisfaction.

"That'll do. Your head took a real pounding in there, so I need to wake you up now and again to make sure you stay with us, but I'll let you rest as much as I dare." Someone helped prop him up. Turning his head to see who it was felt like a truly bad idea. The effort did bring his attention to his arm, though. It had been bandaged and splinted and restrained in a sling.

Adalva held up a small cup for him, and he took its warm, bitter contents in careful sips. "All of it," she insisted. "It'll help with the pain."

"W'happened?"

"At the manor?" she asked. He answered with a ghost of a nod. "That's the question everyone's asking. Don't you worry about it now. It's over. Your only job is to heal."

She was trying to avoid telling him bad news. She might think he didn't know yet about Father, but there were any number of other people she might be putting off telling him about—including both Jane and Venah. Or it could be about the sheer number of people now dead or missing. But he could hardly speak, he could hardly move, and sleep still beckoned.

There seemed little chance now that any bad news would be getting worse while he slept. Jordan let himself sink back down into the bed, and no amount of curiosity or concern could hold off the darkness trying to reclaim him. There were no dreams, just Adalva prodding him awake again.

"Time to move. Can you walk for me?"

Jordan was relieved to find his limbs responding to his will again, just bruised and stiff. The chill had faded enough that he was barely shivering, the pain had faded enough that he didn't feel like he was ramming his head into a wall with each step, and he only felt a deep, aching throb in his splinted arm. There might have been some correlation between that and the way the world had shifted into so many vivid and unnatural colors, or the way that everything sounded like he was hearing it underwater. He hoped those were side-effects of whatever Adalva had given him to drink and not a product of the blows he'd taken to his head.

Once he'd managed a slow circuit of the room, Adalva helped him into his pants that were still warm from drying by the fire and into a pair of overly large boots scrounged from somewhere because, she said, his own were still damp. Then— leaving him wrapped in a blanket instead of struggling with a shirt—she led him out into the piercingly bright sunlight and toward a waiting carriage.

She'd been looking after him in one of the servants' outbuildings on a rise at the edge of the manor grounds. The snow covering the lawn had been largely replaced by an expansive sheet of ice that sparkled in the sun. Most of the outbuildings remained intact, though many—including the chapel—looked to have suffered from flooding. The manor itself had turned into the burned-out hulk he had expected to see.

"Are you good with staying at Montacute for a while, Jordan?" Adalva asked. "While everything gets sorted out?" At his questioning gaze she nodded. "Venah's okay. Well, she will be. She wasn't hurt as badly as you.

"The company will do you both good as you convalesce. Her brother's one of the missing, too. I'm sure she could use help dealing with that." Again, there was the sadness in Adalva's eyes over words unspoken. "They took her on home already."

"Jane?" Jordan managed to ask.

"I..." Adalva hesitated, then nodded over to one of the household knights, who was carrying a limp, heavily wrapped bundle toward a second carriage nearby. "She was hurt bad, Jordan. Really bad. But your sister's a fighter. I'm betting she'll pull through."

At his wide-eyed alarm she just tightened her grip and kept guiding him toward the first carriage. "I know. I know," Adalva said soothingly. "No matter how much of a pain she can be, she's blood, and blood is important. I'll take her straight away to the very best healers. With her mother's reputation in the church, I think I can arrange for her to see an actual miracle worker. I swear I'll keep her alive all the way to Serylia, if that's what it takes."

The words tried to come out in a rush, but all Jordan succeeded in doing was set off a chain reaction that went from flinching from the pain in his jaw, to a spike of agony from jostling his head, to nearly collapsing in the snow before the strong hands of the men escorting them caught him and lifted him into the carriage.

"Hush. Hush." Adalva offered him a reassuring smile. "I'll bring her back good as new before you know it."

The blankets fell partly away as Jane was loaded into her carriage, and Jordan caught a glimpse of her pale arm and face with her eyes open but unfocused. Her hand clutched a partly crumbled gingerbread cookie to her breast like a doll.

It might have been his imagination or Adalva's brew, but for just a moment he thought he saw her eyes flicker and focus malignantly on him while the scent of hot gingerbread spices swirled up out of nowhere. Then the moment was gone. Still cradled limply in the knight's arms and with no hint of focus in her eyes, she was hefted into the carriage and disappeared. The world once again smelled only of snow and horses and scorched timber.

Feeling very alone in the carriage despite the escort that climbed in after him, Jordan watched what remained of his old home disappear behind him while his head filled with questions regarding the manufacture and distribution of horseshoes.

Printed in Dunstable, United Kingdom